"You're not going without me!"

Malinche had had enough of being treated like a child. "I'll follow you if I have to."

Brian hesitated. If she went with him, she'd be in danger. But she wasn't safe here, either. "All right. But don't slow me down. It's going to be tough. I'm not sure you can handle it."

"Don't worry about me. But you'd better go home and get some sleep. We can start early in the morning—"

"I'm not going home."

Her eyes widened. "We *can't* start for Barrow right now—"

"I mean I'm spending the night here. You're not safe alone."

"I appreciate the thought, but I'm afraid you can't stay," she said. "I have only one bed."

Brian's eyes bored into hers. "That'll do...."

ABOUT THE AUTHOR

Marilyn Cunningham has been writing "forever," but it was after she ended her career with the federal government as a policy administrator that she began writing seriously. Since then she has published nearly a dozen novels in the romance genre for Silhouette Intimate Moments and Harper Paperbacks, as well as ten young adult stories for the German market. *Under the Midnight Sun* is her first Intrigue novel.

In 1995 Marilyn was nominated by *Affaire de Coeur* as one of the favorite top ten authors of romance on the basis of a reader poll.

Marilyn lives on ten acres in the mountains of Idaho along with her husband, John, and an assortment of dogs, cats and sheep. Besides her writing, she is passionate about gardening, hiking and reading.

Under the Midnight Sun
Marilyn Cunningham

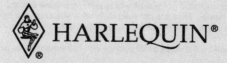

HARLEQUIN®

TORONTO • NEW YORK • LONDON
AMSTERDAM • PARIS • SYDNEY • HAMBURG
STOCKHOLM • ATHENS • TOKYO • MILAN • MADRID
PRAGUE • WARSAW • BUDAPEST • AUCKLAND

To my sons, Bryce and Bruce, who had some definite
ideas as to who the villain should be, and to my
daughter, Cherie, for her constant encouragement.

ISBN 0-373-22492-3

UNDER THE MIDNIGHT SUN

Printed in the U.S.A.

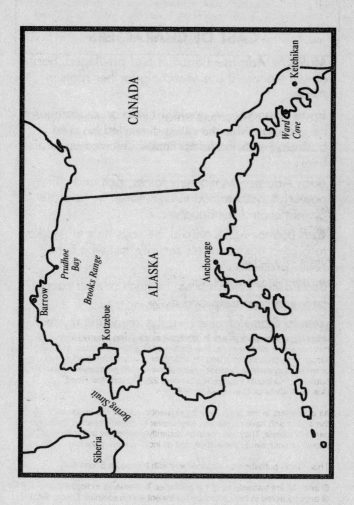

CAST OF CHARACTERS

Malinche Adams—Beautiful and privileged, born of two worlds, she is searching for her roots in Alaska.

Brian Kennedy—A geologist with an oil company, he is a man who has always minded his own business—until he finds himself involved up to his heart.

Buck Adams—Malinche's father, rich and powerful, accustomed to command, he finds he cannot control his daughter.

Carl Bettnor—CIA official, he says he's in Alaska to protect our country's security, but who is he really protecting?

Joe Pasco—Brian's boss, he finds himself caught between friendship and duty.

Dimitri Stanislof—He held the key to the mystery— but someone killed him to keep him quiet....

Prologue

The blizzard was worsening. Tiny particles that had, for over an hour, been slipping through his ski mask to sting Brian Kennedy's face, escalated to needles of pain. Pushed along by a sixty-mile-an-hour wind, they stabbed through the heavy down of his parka and seeped under the guard of fox fur around his face.

Ignoring the discomfort, he willed the snowmobile to keep going. He wasn't far from the shelter of his camp on the shore of the Bering Sea in Alaska, but from what he could see across the gray tundra, he might have been going toward Siberia.

Eskimos had a least fifteen names for snow; during his stint of exploring the Arctic as a geologist for Universal Oil Company, Brian had learned them. Now the only word for what was hitting his face was one he would never use in polite company. He muttered it under his breath.

He squinted, gunmetal gray eyes peering across the monotonous frozen plane. This storm was unusual for early May. The ice should be breaking, the tumultuous display of wildflowers about to begin. When he had started down the coast this morning toward the wildlife refuge, intent on locating possible sites for drilling exploratory holes outside the boundary of the refuge, he hadn't expected this weather. But he should know by now that the Arctic was as unpredictable and untrustworthy as a woman.

He swerved to avoid a small hummock, glanced down at an inert object, and nearly went on. It was only a gray bundle of fur, a fox or caribou, claimed by the implacable Arctic....

Suddenly he caught his breath, and his heart did a jig. He circled around the object, reluctant to admit what he was seeing. At some hidden level of his mind, he had known instantly that it wasn't a fox or caribou, but he had to make sure.

The body, clad in fur, was lying spread-eagled, partially covered by a heavy dusting of snow. Half an hour later and it would have vanished beneath the white blanket. A glance at the broad face, the sightless eyes, the coarse black hair stiff with ice confirmed his instinctive knowledge. An Eskimo or Indian, frozen to death.

Kneeling beside the body, Brian grasped the gloveless hand. It was frozen solid. He let the hand fall back to the ground and glanced around for some means of conveyance, something that might have brought the man to this cold fate, but there was no sled, no snowmobile. Odd that he had been wandering around on foot. Perhaps he'd had a dog sled, and the animals had run away. The blizzard had scoured the frozen ground of all tracks.

Grunting, he hoisted the man up and propped him on the back of the snowmobile. The only thing to do was to get the body to his camp, pack him in his plane, and fly him to Prudhoe Bay, the closest place that might have police or medical facilities. He would let the authorities take it from there. It wasn't his concern.

He glanced back over his shoulder to be sure he hadn't left anything.

It was so tiny he almost missed it. In the depression where the man had lain, his body protecting the ground from the snow, lay a small green object that must have fallen out of his clothes.

Brian picked it up and shoved it in his parka pocket. He'd turn it over to the authorities when he deposited the body.

He was soon over his initial surprise. He considered himself a logical, pragmatic man. It was too bad. He hated waste of any kind, the waste of human life most of all. But things happen, especially in the Arctic, a place unforgiving of mistakes. He had worked for an oil company many places in the world and he considered the Arctic the most unpredictable.

It was odd, though. He wouldn't expect an Eskimo to become lost. Still, it wasn't his problem. He would take the body to Prudhoe Bay and let the authorities handle it.

Brian had lived most of his thirty-three years quite satisfactorily by minding nobody's business but his own. And that's exactly what he would do about this unexpected incident. It had nothing to do with him.

Chapter One

Malinche Adams sat in her expensive wingback chair, long legs curled beneath her, and stared at the letter that had so recently turned her life upside down. She couldn't take her eyes from it, even though the words were burned in her brain.

She had left her affluent life in Seattle only two weeks ago, determined to escape her controlling father—who indulged her shamelessly as long as he made all her decisions—and search for her roots in Alaska. Perhaps her father had been right in considering the move ridiculous. At 32, she was a little old to be searching for her identity. There had been years of false starts, projects that didn't interest her, as she tried to conform to her father's expectations. She desperately needed to get away, find her own path, and when she heard of a job working for a Native corporation in Anchorage, it seemed the answer to her problems. She could use Anchorage as a base while she explored the state of her birth.

It had seemed things might work out. The job was scheduled to begin in a few days, she had a place to live, and was beginning to explore her new city.

Now she realized she had found more than she bargained for.

She thought of how her life had been before she decided to make this move. Her mother had died at her birth, and although she missed having a mother, she hadn't lacked parental love. Buck Adams, her wealthy and influential father, had given her affection as well as privileges. It wasn't his fault that she had always felt different, ill at ease in the private schools she attended, lost in a culture that wasn't quite her own. Buck had always told her she got her exotic coloring, her dark silky hair, her almond eyes, from her Alaskan Native mother, so perhaps she got the feeling of being an outsider in Buck's culture from her mother, too.

Buck. She still seethed with hurt and anger at the way he had reacted to her news.

Soon after she arrived in late April, she'd had a message on her answering machine from a man called Dimitri Stanislof, whom she'd never met, although she knew of him. He was a well-known Native artist, renowned for his carvings of dragons and arctic wildlife. He had sounded excited. He'd said he would see her soon; they had something to talk about.

She'd heard nothing further until she received a package in the mail postmarked from Barrow. It contained a letter from Dimitri. He said he was her half brother. It was so far-fetched that at first she didn't believe it, but the documents he sent confirmed it.

She picked up the letter again and scanned it, although it was already committed to memory. Dimitri hadn't known of the relationship until an old aunt had died and sent him the marriage certificate and birth certificate. His father was Buck Adams, his mother Marie Stanislof. There was no doubt. He said he would see Malinche soon. He had something to take care of first.

A letter from his friend came with the letter. Dimitri was dead, apparently frozen to death on the tundra. He had told his friend he was looking for someone, and he might be in danger. If he didn't return, the friend was to forward his letter and the documents to Malinche.

In one minute she had found a brother and lost him. Dazed, she had called Buck. At first he had evaded her questions, but he finally admitted the truth. Years ago when he was a poor prospector, he had married Marie. They'd had a son. Then she'd left, taking Dimitri, and vanished among her kinsmen.

"But why didn't you do anything?" she'd cried. "Didn't you try to find him? He was your son. And why didn't you tell me?"

"I thought that would hurt you less," he had said. "And I did try to find them, after I struck it rich and had the means to look. I was told they had both died during WWII. And a few years later I married your mother."

"What else haven't you told me?" she demanded. "What about my mother?"

"Tara?" His voice softened. "She died at your birth."

"But what was she like?"

"Like you. Beautiful and brave. If you're wondering if you have any more unknown relatives, I doubt it. She told me she was an orphan. She was an Aleut, like Marie. They looked a lot like each other. Maybe that's why…" His voice trailed away.

"She was an Aleut, but you met her in an Indian village."

"She lived there several years after she left Ward Cove, the detention camp during the war. She wouldn't discuss Ward Cove at all."

He hesitated, then continued. "I know how hard this is, sweetheart, but there's nothing to be done now. Don't get involved."

Still in shock, Malinche had replaced the phone. World War II. It all seemed so long ago. Buck would have been a very young man. He was nearing eighty now. She had been born when he was well into middle life. Perhaps that was why he was so protective even now that she was an adult.

Now Malinche placed the letter back on the stand, still shocked at Buck's betrayal, at a loss as to what to do next. She had always felt so alone, and all the time she'd had a brother. How could he have kept it from her? And now it was too late—Dimitri was dead.

She certainly wasn't going to leave it like this. She had heard on the news of the man who had been found frozen on the tundra, and now realized it had been Dimitri. She felt something was dreadfully wrong about the report. It didn't make sense. Dimitri was at home in the arctic. He wouldn't have wandered around and gotten lost. Besides, his friend had said, and Dimitri had hinted, that whatever he had been involved in was dangerous. He had been afraid.

The more she thought of it, the clearer it became. It wasn't an accident. Dimitri had been killed. Murdered. She thought of everything she had missed by not knowing her brother—the long, intimate talks, the feeling of family—and her heart ached with loss.

She stood up, so blinded by tears that she almost knocked over the end table. She'd had time to think since the letter came. Buck's admonition to let it drop only fueled her intent. She wouldn't let whoever had killed Dimitri get away with it. She would find the truth. Her brother's death had been written off as an accident, and no one was pursuing justice.

The first thing she would do would be to call the police. She picked up the phone. A few minutes later she put it down, shaking her head in disbelief. She'd had trouble even getting them to admit they had identified the body as Dimitri's. And they insisted it was an accident. No further action was even being contemplated.

At this point, further talks with the police seemed unproductive, at least until she knew more. The logical place to begin was with the man who found the body. The newspaper had given his name—Brian Kennedy. And he lived right here in Anchorage. A quick look through the phone book gave her his address.

She closed her eyes and murmured softly, meaning it to the depth of her being, "I won't forget you, Dimitri. I won't give up. I'll find whoever killed you, and bring them to justice."

AT THE PEAL of the doorbell, Brian glanced up from the fishing fly he was painstakingly tying and frowned. He wasn't expecting anyone, and he wasn't anxious to see anyone. He had been back in his Anchorage apartment for a week; now he planned to spend a few days trout fishing in a remote lake, then go down to Cabo San Lucas to bask in the sun. An unexpected visitor wasn't going to mess up his plans.

He unwound his legs from the chair and moved reluctantly toward the door, glancing at his watch. Ten in the evening. An odd hour for company.

He opened the door and felt a jolt to his solar plexus.

Suddenly fish were the last thing on his mind. A woman he had never met was standing at the door. A gorgeous woman.

She was dramatically beautiful. Above average in height, she had only to tilt her head upward a fraction of an inch and her deep brown eyes, almond-shaped, met his. Black silky hair fell ruler straight to her shoulders. Her generous mouth, straight nose, and high cheekbones were sculpted with crisp clarity, and his breath caught as his eyes lingered on the long, graceful line of her throat.

He was overreacting; he'd been out in the bush too long.

"Brian Kennedy?" Her voice was low, with an enticing lilt.

"That's me." He'd gotten control of himself. Beautiful though she was, he still didn't want her messing up his plans, and he had a hunch that was exactly what she would try to do.

"Well—may I come in?"

"Sure." Shrugging, he stood back and motioned her inside, alarm bells ringing. Her clothing might have been meant to be casual, but there was nothing casual about the shimmering silk material of her pale yellow shirt, and her jeans fit far too lovingly to have been bought off the rack. The blue jacket slung over her shoulders was obviously expensive; her running shoes were top of the line. She walked with an easy grace that came from being accustomed to the best.

He knew the type. Plenty of money, spoiled rotten.

Inside his small living room, he watched her quick survey of his quarters and caught her small frown. So, the lady was used to something better. Too bad.

"It's not luxurious," he said, "but I like it."

"What?"

"The apartment. You were frowning."

And he did like it. He kept it neat, and that meant no extraneous objects. A comfortably worn sofa, an upholstered chair, shelves of books, a rustic coffee table topped with rocks and minerals—what more could one want?

The sharpness of his tone caught her attention. "I didn't mean to offend you. I just have something else on my mind...."

She turned and offered her hand. She had a surprisingly firm grip. "I'm Malinche Adams."

"What can I do for you?"

"Well, you could ask me to sit down. This may take a while."

"Oh, sorry." It wouldn't take too long, he hoped, motioning her to the sofa. Her carriage, her voice, her clothes, all spoke of money, which Brian had found usually meant a determination to have one's own way. He scooped some books from a chair and sat across from her, waiting expectantly.

She seemed to have a problem as to how to begin. "I have some questions for you," she finally said. "You found Dimitri Stanislof, didn't you?"

"Dimitri Stanislof?" He shook his head; he didn't recall anyone by that name. Although it did sound somewhat familiar.

"The man you found frozen to death on the slope. The police told me you found the body and brought him to Prudhoe Bay."

"Oh, sure." He nodded, remembering. "A couple of weeks ago. But Dimitri Stanislof? I thought the man I found was an Eskimo."

"He was an Aleut. A lot of Aleuts have Russian

names, from the time the Russian fur traders took over the Aleutian Islands.''

"What do you want to know, Malinche?"

She lifted her eyes to his. Riveting brown eyes, he thought, suddenly uneasy. They looked misty, suspiciously as though she were about to cry. "They said he got lost and froze to death."

"That's the way it looked to me."

"That wouldn't have happened to Dimitri!" She jumped up from the sofa and paced a few steps across the narrow room. "He was a Native. He knew the territory. Even if that snowstorm was unusual, it would come as no surprise to him. Did they mention how he got there?"

Brian frowned. That bothered him a little, too. "So what do *you* think happened?"

She sighed and collapsed again on the sofa. "I think somebody killed him."

Brian stared at her. "That's quite an accusation."

"It's the only thing that makes sense," she said stubbornly.

He had been right; she was going to be a problem. "I gather the authorities don't think so. Maybe he was hunting and didn't realize how far he'd gone."

"He wasn't a hunter. He was an artist. And a very good one."

An artist. Was that why the name sounded familiar? He'd had to answer some questions about the body, but he didn't recall the authorities mentioning the man's identity, if they had known at the time.

"An artist could get lost more easily than a hunter."

He leaned back in his chair, still skeptical, not only about her story, but her motives as well. What was this affair to her? He had to admit he'd been curious about the guy, more curious than he had admitted even to himself. That didn't mean he wanted to be involved.

"Suppose you tell me why you're so sure he was killed. And while you're at it, what's your interest in him? So far, it doesn't add up."

"There was something more." She hesitated, as though unsure how far to trust him, then apparently made up her mind. Haltingly, searching for words, she told him about the message on her answering machine and the package she had received. "You see, I have a duty to him. Dimitri was my brother."

He lifted an eyebrow, but didn't say anything for a moment. "I'm sorry," he said finally. "But what do you want from me?"

She leaned toward him, eyes glowing with eagerness. "Did you find anything, see anything, that you didn't tell the police about?"

He hated to quench the hope in her eyes, but he couldn't think of a thing. Everything had been chaos when he brought the body in. People running around, giving terse instructions, making calls. He had gotten away as quickly as he could.

But wait. There was something forgotten in the confusion. He moved to his parka and took out the tiny green object. He had completely forgotten about it. Only later, at home, when he'd put his hand in his pocket had he remembered. As yet, he hadn't gotten around to giving it to the police. He extended his arm and opened his fist. "This was lying under the body."

She gasped. "It's a Dimitri dragon."

He scrutinized the object more carefully. The delicately carved dragon had a spiny tail and four clawed toes on each of its four feet. The body twisted in a sinister shape. Every detail was expertly worked from the forked tail to the tongue half out of the wide-open mouth. Brian felt the power of the intricately carved object.

But there was something strange about the head. It had an eerie, half-human look....

"A dragon?" He echoed. "I thought Natives carved seals and polar bears—things like that."

She shook her head. "Dimitri was obsessed with dragons. I've seen several of his exhibits, and there's always a dragon...it was his trademark. In the brochures I've read, he said he'd carved them all his life. There's probably a Dimitri dragon in every tourist shop in town."

Her fingers clutched the dragon, and she gazed beseechingly at him. Brian's fingers trembled. He actually had to close his fist to keep from reaching over and smoothing his hands down over the black silk of her hair, lifting it off her neck to watch it flow like dark water through his hands. The sensation was distinctly unwelcome. Women like her were trouble, soft, unfit for the North. Immediately he wondered why he cared. Instead, he closed her fingers over the dragon. It was hers by right.

Her mouth trembled. "Will you help me find out who killed him? You found his body, you've talked to the police. You'll know who I should talk to first."

"No." Brian's rejection might not have been so brusque if she didn't affect him so strongly. "Besides, why me? The police must have a reason for thinking the death was an accident. And if you're determined not to drop it, why not talk to his friends? There must be someone who'll help."

"I'm going to talk to whoever I can locate, but I doubt they'll be of help with the police so adamant that it was an accident. Besides, you did find the body, took it to the authorities. You might not have noticed anything at the time, but you might remember something strange if you look back.''

''What about the body? Where is it?''

''They haven't released it yet. Said they had another test or two to do.''

That was strange, Brian mused to himself. But it still wasn't any of his business. ''I didn't notice anything,'' Brian reiterated. ''The police took only a brief statement from me. I didn't even know who I'd found until now. It's nothing to me.''

''I'll pay…''

Pay! It figured she would think that anything could be purchased. A spoiled woman, used to her own way. He glared at her, angry that she had aroused such a warm sensation in him. ''No. I'm not for sale. And it's none of my business. I'd advise you to forget about it, too.''

''Advise?'' Her chin came up. ''I don't recall asking for your advice.''

''Look, I stay out of things that don't concern me. And if you're smart, you won't go around telling everyone your suspicions. Just go on home and forget it.''

''Forget it?'' She glared at him. ''So, you won't help me. You still can't tell me what to do. I don't need your patronizing *advice!*''

She whirled, grabbed her jacket from the back of the couch, and strode out the door. The closing slam reverberated through Brian's apartment and down his spine to the small of his back.

MALINCHE CLOSED HER EYES, leaned back against his door, and took several slow, calming breaths. Why was she reacting so strongly? His words hadn't really been that offensive. No, but he had been so sure he knew what was right for her, had tried to order her around just as Buck did. She hadn't come all the way to Alaska just to find another controlling male.

Yet she had to admit something about him had attracted her immediately. He wasn't incredibly handsome, if you were talking about classical features. His strong nose was a bit off center, probably broken in a fight. His firm jaw looked determined, even pugnacious. He wasn't a man to be pushed around.

Well, she wasn't a woman to be pushed around, either. And did he really know as little about Dimitri, about what the authorities had found, as he said? He had found the body, he had given a statement. Wasn't he the least bit curious?

She shoved her hands in her pockets, shook her hair back from her face and stepped out onto the sidewalk. She would walk the mile and a half to her apartment. Brian's refusal to help wasn't the only thing causing her despondent mood. She had thought that when she got to Alaska things would be simpler, and that she would finally feel that she belonged someplace, but she was as much a stranger here as she had been in those snooty schools her dad had persisted in sending her to. Schools where she had felt hopelessly out of place, where people spoke a cultural language she didn't understand.

Perhaps it was natural to feel alienated. She'd never known her mother. She had lived her first seven years in the safe, enclosed world of a Native village where Buck had left her while he prospected for gold. She'd been loved and cossetted by everyone. Then Buck Adams, dreamer and prospector, had struck it rich, remembered he had a child, and her life had changed irrevocably.

She knew she wasn't entitled to sympathy for having a rich, indulgent—and autocratic—father, but the change in her life had been dramatic. She could have anything she wanted—except a feeling of belonging.

She wondered if she should go to the villagers for help, but it had been years since she'd been in contact with anyone from the village. She might not know anyone who lived there now. And they were simple people, not likely to have much influence with the authorities.

There was also Dimitri's friend, the one who had sent her the letter. She would talk to him later, but she still thought since Brian had found the body, had talked to the police, he was the logical place to begin. She had made a few inquiries about him and he seemed well-known in the state—and well-connected.

Deep in thought, she lowered her head and kept her eyes on the sidewalk, hardly aware of the cars passing, the occasional pedestrian walking briskly along.

She glanced up, suddenly aware that traffic had thinned. A shiver of uneasiness skittered down her back; she still wasn't used to the solitude one sometimes found in Anchorage.

Then she relaxed. Anchorage wasn't that far from the arctic circle. Even though it was late, the sky still retained a soft, golden light; the summer days were as endless as the winter nights. Of course there was no traffic. Everyone was probably home in bed.

There was one car, though, driving slowly behind her. Although she hadn't been consciously aware of it, she realized now it had been there for several minutes.

Unable to stop herself, she glanced back over her

shoulder. The car slowed even more, then pulled up to the curb and parked a couple of hundred feet behind her. She sighed with relief. Obviously, the driver had been driving slowly looking for an address.

Her thoughts swung back to Dimitri, the brother that she would never know. The loss stung, brought tears to her eyes. She was his only hope for justice; she couldn't let him down. The police maintained it was an accident, and at this point she had nothing but intuition telling her it wasn't.

She was passing a vacant lot now. The landscaped yards of houses had given way to a thick stand of alpine fir underplanted with thick brush. She shivered. This strange northern night, with its faint, wavering illumination, wasn't at all the familiar light of daytime. It was more like twilight, an in-between time, a time that encouraged fears and fantasy. That must be the reason her neck was tingling and she felt as though someone were staring at her back.

She heard the screech of tires. With her heart slamming against her chest, she whirled. The car had pulled out from the curb and was speeding down the street toward her.

Why was it coming so fast? It was almost upon her! And it was swerving toward her!

For an instant she was immobilized with fear. A few details burned themselves into her mind. It was a late model sedan. The windshield was tinted. She could only see a dark silhouette behind the wheel.

Then everything seemed to happen in slow motion. The vehicle was only a few feet away but it seemed to take forever to cover the space. Breaking her paralysis, she jumped backward, feeling herself moving as slowly as though she were swimming in molasses.

She didn't feel the impact of the fender slam against her leg. She only knew she was flying through endless time. Then everything went black.

Chapter Two

The pontoons touched lightly, and Brian taxied across the mirrorlike lake to the pier where he tethered his small Cessna. The fishing trip had been a mistake; he couldn't keep his mind on it and after three days finally admitted he didn't care whether he caught a trout or not.

The problem was Malinche; he couldn't get her out of his mind. And it was ridiculous. Even the damned woman's name was ridiculous. He had always prided himself on his ability to control his life, to stay clear of the sentimental impulses that most people seemed prone to, and he didn't like this development.

Malinche seemed all emotion. Certainly she had a temper. The slamming door still echoed in his ears. He'd resisted an impulse to run after her. At least see she got home safely.

And get yourself involved in something you don't want, he thought. He'd met women like Malinche. They were a hazard of the North—rich, spoiled women who thought a rugged Alaskan man would be a good diversion. A trophy. But when things got tough they couldn't hack it. He'd met one in particular—had a beautiful summer that meant more to him than it did to her—and she'd left with the first hard frost. An Alaskan man might look glamorous, but the hard facts of arctic life soon wore the glamour away.

Yet something had been worrying him ever since Malinche had insisted Dimitri had been murdered. It was the first time he had wondered if there might be a connection to the bizarre things that had been happening to him. He was sure his apartment had been searched, he'd felt that he was being followed, and there was that strange message on his answering machine: "We know you have it. We'll be in touch." Wrong number, he'd thought. He had no explanation. There was nothing in his place to steal, and the cryptic message meant absolutely nothing. But if Dimitri really had been murdered...and someone thought he knew something...

Unless it was that silly dragon. If so, he couldn't see why. Malinche had said her brother had carved dozens of them, that there was probably one in every shop in town.

He took his backpack from the plane, walked up the pier to where his Jeep was parked. He jumped into the vehicle and headed down the steep, winding road toward Anchorage, driving perhaps a little faster than he should.

It happened on the first turn. He braked, and the pedal hit the floor. The Jeep was headed right off the road into a ravine. Fear and surprise stabbed him. Desperately he fought for control. He bounced off the shoulder, turned the wheel into the bank. The resulting crash shook him up, but at least he was still alive.

He climbed out of the Jeep and scooted under the frame. As he'd suspected, the brake lines had been severed. Cursing, he radioed for a tow truck and sat on the side of the road going over what had happened. It was becoming too obvious to explain away. Someone wanted him out of the way, and they were serious. Only luck had kept him from ending up in the ravine.

The only thing out of the ordinary that he'd done recently had been to find Dimitri's body. A cold chill went down his back. Perhaps someone thought he'd reached Dimitri before he died. And that Dimitri had talked. If Dimitri had been murdered, that would explain these bizarre incidents. He was a threat.

Arriving finally at his apartment, he threaded the key into the lock, then paused. The door wasn't locked. He was sure he had locked it. Gingerly, he entered the room, then halted, his gaze sweeping beyond the foyer to the living area. He whistled softly. He'd thought someone had searched his apartment before. This time it was definite. Someone had taken the place apart.

He stood for a moment, breathing heavily, fists clenched. He didn't care much about material objects, but the invasion of his privacy infuriated him. He made a quick search. It appeared nothing had been taken. Putting back the cushions that had been ripped from his couch, he sat down and contemplated the situation. Things were piling up. The accident with the Jeep might well mean that whoever had searched his apartment hadn't found what they wanted and had decided to eliminate him.

He went out into the hall and rapped sharply on his landlady's door. It opened immediately.

"Brian." Mrs. Lindsay's rotund face creased into a cheery smile. "I wasn't expecting you back for a few days." She broke off, her eyes suddenly anxious. "Is anything wrong?"

"Horrible!" she interjected, as he outlined what had happened. "Did they take anything?"

"Not that I can tell. Did you hear anything?"

Mrs. Lindsay flushed. "No—but then, I go to sleep early."

Brian didn't pursue it. Mrs. Lindsay liked a few nips of whisky at bedtime. Probably the place could have tumbled down around her and she wouldn't have heard a thing.

She reached behind her and picked up several papers from a table by the door. "I brought your papers in."

He thanked her and went back to his apartment. He should call the police, but he doubted there was anything they could do. Certainly not, if he was right about the reason for the break-in.

Several hours later he had his apartment back in shape, but he was too restless to relax. He decided to call his boss and tell him he was back in town. Joe Pasco, a middle manager at Universal Oil, was also his friend.

"Brian! Glad you're back." Pasco's voice boomed across the wire. "So, all that nature finally got to you. I never could figure out why a man who makes his living in the wilderness would go there for a vacation."

"Just perverse, I guess," Brian replied, grinning. There was no explaining the pull of the vast solitude, the sheer joy of being alone on the tundra with the electrical extravaganza of the northern lights flickering overhead, the haunting cry of a wolf in his ears. "Besides, I'll have enough sun and sand in Mexico. Anything happen while I was gone?"

"Nah, same old stuff. Some of the Native groups are kicking up a fuss about that new oil field we want to drill."

"Serious?"

"Probably not. Many of them know the benefits oil has brought."

"Anymore information about that guy I carted into Prudhoe?"

A slight hesitation. "Not that I heard about. Universal Oil wasn't involved, except to hand him over to the authorities. Don't find any more dead bodies, Brian. Too much paperwork. You should have my job—you'd find out what work is."

Brian laughed. It was an old discussion. He could have been well up the corporate ladder now, but he insisted on staying in the field. He couldn't see giving up freedom for money.

"I almost forgot," Pasco continued. "There was one thing. Somebody was around here asking about you—where you were, if you were the guy who found the dead stiff up on the tundra. Real nosy."

Brian was instantly alert. "Who was he?"

"I didn't talk to him. The receptionist told me about it. And she's on vacation."

After a few more lighthearted comments, Brian hung up the phone, frowning. No one had any reason to be asking about him at work. He didn't like the way things were stacking up.

Abandoning the conjecture, he began leafing through the newspapers Mrs. Lindsay had saved for him. He was well into the second, when the item leaped right out at him. Pulse racing, he read the item once, then carefully reread it.

Woman Victim of Hit-and-Run Accident
Miss Malinche Adams was taken to University Hospital yesterday evening, the victim of a hit-

and-run accident on Muldoon Street. She was treated for shock and bruises and released. Police are looking for a dark, late-model sedan with tinted windows.

The paper dropped from his nerveless hand. The poor girl. All alone, no friends, and probably scared to death. The paper didn't give an address, and it wasn't likely the hospital would release it. Brian, however, rarely worried about official sources. A quick call to an acquaintance who worked in hospital administration, and within twenty minutes, he had shaved, showered, put on a clean shirt and jeans, and was in his loaner Jeep.

As he sped along the street, rueful knowledge of his own motives vied with his anxiety. He'd been waiting for something, any excuse, to see her. A woman he didn't trust as far as he could throw her.

AT THE SOUND of the doorbell, Malinche's heart raced. The doorbell triggered fear—fear that was always lurking in the shadows of her mind since her accident. Her encounter with the speeding vehicle had left her downright paranoid. She had lived all her life without encountering malice or danger, and their obvious presence in the form of a car bent on harming her had changed her view of life.

Adding to her fear was her sense that someone was watching her. There was nothing specific, but she thought a car had been parked outside today longer than it should have been; it left when she opened the door and stared at it. And there had been footsteps in the night. Once she had answered the phone to hear only a buzzing tone.

With the chain still in place, she opened the door a few inches.

A jolt of pure pleasure and relief coursed through her. Although she had certainly thought about him, she hadn't expected to see Brian Kennedy again—at least not standing at her door looking fit and competent and totally in command. He had been so adamant in refusing to help her, had made it so clear that he couldn't wait to get rid of her, that he was the last person she expected to see.

She hesitated a fraction of a second. What reason had she to trust Brian? She had been on her way home from his apartment when the automobile had run her down. And she still thought he knew more about Dimitri's death than he was telling. But just a look into those wide-spaced, intelligent gray eyes made her suspicions seem insane.

On the other hand, she wasn't overlooking the fact that he had refused to help her, had even said she was snooping into things that were none of her affair. He had ordered her to stop, believing he could tell her what to do. He needn't think she would forget that just because he showed up at her door.

"Hello, Mr. Kennedy. What can I do for you?" Ice tinkled in her voice. She was ridiculously glad to see him, but he didn't have to know it.

"It was Brian before," he said. "May I come in?" After a moment, she stepped aside and let him in. His presence seemed to fill the living room with masculine energy, overpowering the slim lines of the Edwardian couch, making the glass-topped coffee table with the delicate brass legs appear fragile, almost ephemeral. When he sat down on the wingback chair he seemed completely composed, although he seemed to have trouble with where to put his hands. Was he just a little nervous himself?

Good.

She glanced around the room, trying to see it through his eyes. Even in decorating a room she was torn, with antiques juxtaposed with modern pieces, an abstract painting against peach-colored walls, the stiff couch resting on the plush off-white, wall-to-wall carpeting. She wasn't at all sure of her taste. It all came together in pleasing harmony, but she couldn't quite see how.

"I read about your accident," Brian said. "I came as soon as I heard. Were you badly hurt?"

"Not really—just shaken up a bit." In spite of her determination to keep him at arm's length, she was touched by his concern. "It's been a few days, and I'm over the worst of it."

He grinned at her obvious reference to the fact that he hadn't come as immediately as he'd said. "I've been out of town. I'm glad it wasn't serious. Do you have someone to stay with you?"

"I wasn't badly hurt. I don't need anyone."

His smile challenged her statement. "So, you're a woman who can take care of herself. I'm impressed."

"I've always taken care of myself, made my own decisions." Not true, not when Buck was around. But she would make it true now.

"That's a shame. No candidates for the job?"

"Are you applying?" Damn him. Now he had her flirting.

"I'm not much for full-time employment," he said, grinning. "But you could certainly make me consider it, if anyone could."

"Don't do me any favors."

"Malinche," he mused. "That's a very unusual name."

She shrugged. "Blame my father. He's a romantic. Malinche was the name of Cortez's Native wife. Since my mother was part Aleut, I guess he thought it appropriate."

"I think he was right. It has an exotic, mysterious flavor, like you. Isn't she the one who betrayed her people for love of Cortez?"

"So some people say," she said coldly. "I wouldn't know. If she did, I suspect she had little choice. I can only assure you that I wouldn't do a thing like that."

"Of course not." His curious glance told her she had spoken too emphatically. "It was just an observation."

Again she regretted her hasty words. He had no way of knowing her inner turmoil about her heritage, how she longed to find her roots, know who she was. And he, macho and always in command, would never know the feeling.

"Are you sure you're all right?"

"Of course." With an unconscious gesture, she fingered the bruise on her forehead, and a soft wince escaped her lips.

Brian sprang to his feet. Placing his hands on her shoulders, he moved her directly into the light flooding in the bank of windows. She closed her eyes, feeling her anxiety slip away. This was dangerous, but she basked in his concern.

Scowling, he examined the bruise, brushing her hair back from her forehead, moving his fingers over her temple. She caught his scent, musky, masculine. To her chagrin, her aches faded into the background, and she was aware of feelings much more pleasurable.

He must have felt it, too. He stepped back quickly, almost as though he had been stung. "That's a nasty bruise." His voice was low and warm. "Exactly what happened? A drunk driver?"

"That's what the police believe."

"But you don't?" Brian's gaze held hers as firmly as his hands had done a moment ago. It provoked an equally unsettling feeling.

She took a deep breath and turned to stare out the window, considering her reply. Brian already thought she imagined things; he had implied that when she had asked his help in finding out who had killed Dimitri. But she might as well try.

"I told you what I think," she said coolly. "I think I may be getting close to stepping on someone's toes."

"You connect this attack on you with the death of your brother?" He didn't sound as disbelieving as she'd expected.

"It's possible."

"Yes," he said slowly. "You've been asking a lot of questions." He frowned. "Did you stop to think that if you're right, it could be dangerous?"

"It already *is* dangerous!"

To her surprise, he didn't dispute her. He hesitated, then said slowly, "Maybe I should find out a little more...."

Was there actually a chance he might take her concerns seriously? "I think," she said slowly, "that whoever ran me down meant it. He wasn't a random drunk. I think he followed me from your apartment. What's more, I think he meant to do more than frighten me— I think he meant to kill me. It was just luck that I managed to jump out of the way."

She squeezed her eyes shut and hugged her chest,

hearing again the roar of the engine, seeing the horror of the vehicle speeding directly toward her. She couldn't repress a shiver.

Brian placed his hand on her arm, and ushered her gently to the couch. She was acutely aware of his warm hand on her bare flesh.

"Let me fix you a cup of tea," he said. "Then we'll talk."

Brian headed toward the kitchen before she could protest. In a few minutes he was back with a teapot and two fragile porcelain cups that looked impossibly delicate in his strong hands.

"I couldn't find any real tea. Just herbal."

She smiled, feeling much better. She could no more picture Brian drinking herbal tea by preference than she could envision him in a velvet smoking jacket.

"Sorry," she murmured. "That's all I drink."

He seated himself across from her and waited until she took a steadying sip. He left his own cup untouched on the table.

"Well," he finally said, "it sounds like you've been real busy. Stirring up a lot of trouble for yourself. How about telling me everything that's been going on—in detail."

When she finished her recital, he gave a low whistle. "So, you've been to the cops, the FBI, and everybody else with your suspicions. What did they tell you?"

"Not much. They're all very sympathetic, but they just keep insisting there's nothing to show he didn't freeze to death. They all sound like they're reading from the same script. You agree then, that there may be a connection with my digging, and the man who tried to run me down?"

"It's beginning to look that way." He admitted it

reluctantly and she wondered if there was something he wasn't telling her.

"You said we should ask some more questions," she reminded him.

"I said *I* should." He picked up the phone from the table beside the chair and punched in some numbers. "I have a friend in the police department who owes me a couple of favors."

For several minutes Malinche listened to one side of a terse conversation. Then Brian slowly replaced the instrument, a perplexed frown on his face.

"My friend works in the homicide division. He's usually forthcoming with me, but today he'd give a clam a run for his money, but I got a little out of him. You were right about some things."

"What was that?"

"They identified the body, but they're keeping it as quiet as they can. Your brother didn't freeze to death. Not when someone attacked him with a sharp, thin instrument."

She sucked in her breath, feeling her brother's pain deep inside herself. From what she'd heard of Dimitri she felt she would have loved him, treasured him. And to die so horribly. Someone would pay.

"But why wouldn't they tell me?" She forced the words out through her tight throat. "Have they found out anything about who did it?"

Brian stretched out his long legs and contemplated the tips of his boots. "They're keeping everything hushed up. The official story is that Dimitri froze to death—I had to pry out the rest. Because they haven't released the body, I believe they know a lot more than they're saying. From what my friend hinted, I suspect they're under a lot of pressure to keep the lid on. Dimitri must have been involved in something pretty big.''

"But involved in what? He was an artist, not a politician—although I did hear he was opposed to drilling for oil on Native lands. But that would hardly justify murder.''

"And I don't see my employers as murderers, although I suspect if he was an activist, they aren't sorry he's out of action." Brian paced a few steps across the carpet, hands in his pockets, head down. "It's true the oil companies and the environmentalists are going head-to-head over drilling, and it would help if someone as influential as Dimitri was out of the way. But they wouldn't go this far.''

"Wouldn't they?" She couldn't suppress her suspicion. Brian worked for Universal Oil. How far would he go to protect them?

"No," he said shortly. She thought from his expression he wasn't too sure of that. "How about the Natives? Dimitri must have been a thorn in the side of those who wanted the drilling. Everyone isn't committed to a survival life-style."

He turned and placed his hand on her shoulder. "I'm going to check out a few things. Don't leave the house. Call me if anything unusual happens."

Very slowly, as though he hadn't at all meant to do it, he lowered his head and placed his lips gently on hers. She felt the contact down to her toes, the warm, sweet rush of desire she didn't want to feel for him, a man who seemed to have everything under control, including her. A man whom she suspected was keeping a secret from her. With a supreme effort, she broke the contact.

"Sorry," he said, his voice hoarse. "I shouldn't

have done that. There are a few things I need to check on—I'll be in touch.''

At the door he hesitated, as though about to say something. What he said wasn't what she expected. ''Be sure to keep your doors locked.''

''Don't worry about that.''

She watched him vault into the Jeep and drive off, tires spitting gravel. She felt bereft, more shaken than she could admit. At least he was on her side, and he would help her. But why? What wasn't he telling her? Why the sudden change of heart?

His kiss had been more than unsettling. She had wanted him, with a hard desperate desire she'd never felt before. And she wouldn't give in to it. Even when he was leaving he'd given her an order, expected that she'd follow it, as though she had no reasoning ability of her own. She wouldn't go from one man who treated her as a child directly to another. She had to find her own identity.

BRIAN, driving distractedly down the road, still felt the imprint of the kiss. Her lips were so soft, so giving. What had got into him? He'd been burned before. Of course he wasn't silly enough to believe all women were alike—but there were types. Rich, beautiful young women who'd never been denied anything, full of romantic ideas that faded when faced with harsh reality. He didn't need another heartbreak.

He should stay away, but it looked like he had no choice but to dig into this Dimitri thing. Someone had seen to that. Even if he stopped now, there was no assurance the incidents would stop. He wished he knew what they wanted from him, but so far it appeared they just wanted him dead.

And he had to admit he was curious. Why had his friend in the police department been so evasive? And did his boss, Joe Pasco, really know so little? Pasco must have made inquiries about who was asking for Brian. There might be a connection between whoever was snooping around at work and the trashing of his apartment.

And there must have been talk. Universal Oil officials had been in Prudhoe Bay when he'd brought Dimitri's body in.

It seemed someone was doing more than trying to frighten both him and Malinche. These people were serious. They wanted them dead.

Brian believed in the preemptive strike. He wasn't going to sit around and wait for someone to kill him. He had to get to the bottom of this—and quickly.

Chapter Three

Completely frustrated, Brian sat on his couch and ran his fingers through his hair. He'd made a few calls after he got home and was certain now that everyone was covering up, but he was no closer to finding out why. And he couldn't help wondering if Malinche was covering up, too. Her story, if true, was certainly strange.

His apartment seemed quiet, much quieter than the endless slopes of the tundra, because the silence inside was accentuated by the sound of cars outside, the shouts of kids in the park…he could even hear the tick of the clock, his heart thudding.

Damn, he was lonely, and it was all her fault. He reached for the newspaper, and settled back.

Suddenly the door burst open, slammed violently against the wall.

Brian froze. He hadn't heard a thing, had no warning at all. He could do nothing but stare. Then, his paralysis left him as quickly as it had come.

''What the hell!'' He sprang to his feet, half into a crouch, fists clenched, muscles coiled to attack.

A man stood outlined in the doorway. At first glance, he didn't seem too intimidating—close-cropped gray hair, a lined face. Brian thought he might be in his late sixties, perhaps even seventy. Although certainly a well preserved seventy—there were muscles on this man. He gave the impression of strength in the arrogant way he stood: legs spread as though he owned the world, meaty hands clenched. He fixed Brian with a cold stare.

Brian balanced lightly on the balls of his feet, poised to explode toward the intruder. He wished his gun was in his hand instead of on the stand in his bedroom.

"Relax." The man moved into the room, his eyes cataloguing it in one glance. Brian moved forward. This was no ordinary thief; he was much too sure of himself, much too focused. But damned if Brian was going to be ordered around in his own apartment.

"Hold it." The voice was deep, authoritative, a voice used to barking commands.

In spite of himself, Brian paused.

"You should lock your door," the man said, crossing to a chair and seating himself. "You never know who might come in."

"Most people would knock."

Now that the man was seated, Brian's adrenaline was seeping away. He was still angry, but also curious. There was purpose behind the stranger's cold eyes.

He took his time scrutinizing the intruder who lounged so casually in his chair. Or appeared to lounge. Brian was aware that the man's every muscle was rigid under his carefully relaxed pose. The guy was a loaded gun, cocked and ready.

Although of medium height, the intruder was strongly muscled. At his apparent age, he'd obviously lived an active life. Something about him didn't seem to go with the expensive gray-striped suit that was obviously custom-made.

It was the eyes, though, that riveted Brian's attention. Pale blue, almost colorless. Looking into them was like peering into fathomless depths of—nothing. Brian had faced many dangers in his various assignments around the world, but he had never felt this uneasiness prickling along his spine. It wasn't the man's physical appearance that made him appear so lethal. Brian sensed something dangerous in his manner, something that made him think this man was no stranger to violence.

To dispel his uneasiness or to prove he wasn't intimidated—he took a step toward the man, hands on hips. "I don't like people busting in on me. You've got some explaining to do."

"I just came to offer you some advice, Kennedy."

"I like to know who I'm talking to."

"It's not important."

"To me it is," Brian replied. "Start talking, beginning with who in the hell you are—or get out."

The man rose from his chair, eyes slitted. "You're in no position to demand anything—"

Brian sprang forward. One fist connected with the square chin, making a satisfying thud. The man fell backward, his expression registering surprise as he stumbled to his knees.

He rose slowly, frowning, but made no move to retaliate. "You've got guts. Too bad you don't also have a lick of sense."

Glancing at Brian's set jaw, he sank back down in his chair. "You've made your point. Maybe I didn't need to make such a dramatic entrance. I wanted to get your attention, convince you that what I have to say is important."

"Which is?"

"You've been nosing around some dangerous

places." He paused, then shot the words out between thin lips. "What's your interest in Dimitri Stanislof?"

Dimitri Stanislof again, Brian thought. A lot of interest in an ordinary Native, even if he was—or had been—a well-known artist. "What business is it of yours?"

"You've been asking questions. It could get dangerous," the man said softly.

Brian suspected this man knew it already had gotten dangerous. "I found the body, brought it to the authorities. That's all I know."

"Not quite, I think. You'd do well to tell me everything."

"Are you threatening me?"

"I'm warning you, for your own good. You've already discovered that the man was killed. It could be contagious."

"Get out."

The man rose slowly to his feet. "Okay, so you don't scare. I was afraid of that. I didn't want to tell you any more than you had to know. But you're a patriotic man, and I'm sure you wouldn't do anything to harm your country."

He flipped open a wallet and held it in front of Brian's eyes. "Carl Bettnor, CIA."

Brian's mouth dropped open. So, this was an official visit. He suspected the man was acting true to form and wasn't an immediate threat. Brian had worked all over the world. He'd run into CIA types before. This man's tactics of surprise and intimidation weren't unusual.

And CIA involvement explained a few things—the evasiveness, the denials. Everyone would keep a low profile, try to stay out of trouble.

Thinking back on his conversation with his boss, he realized that Pasco might have been trying to warn him. Why? Because Pasco knew of CIA involvement and didn't want trouble? Or because Dimitri was a threat that Universal Oil itself had taken care of?

"What's any of that got to do with me, Bettnor?"

"This Stanislof was involved in some pretty dirty business. And whoever killed him is still out there."

"What was he involved in? From what I heard, he was a harmless artist. I might not agree with his efforts to stop oil drilling, but as a 'patriot,' I know it's within the law to protest."

"He was into a lot more than that."

"Like what?"

"It's government business," Bettnor said firmly. "It involves national security. And remember—whoever killed him is still loose and dangerous. So stay out of it. That's an order."

Bettnor paused, his mouth tightening. "And keep that Adams woman on a short rein, if you have any regard for her."

Without waiting for a reply, Bettnor strode to the door. With his hand on the knob, he turned. "There are people out there who aren't playing games. I think you know that by now. You'd be wise to cooperate, tell what you know." He shut the door firmly behind him.

Brian moved to the door and turned the lock, cold anger growing inside him. CIA or not, the guy had no right to burst in here, spouting threats. The whole scene was designed to intimidate him, nothing else.

Well, it wasn't going to work. No one was going to push him around. But what did he know that someone would kill for? Did they think he had reached Dimitri while he was still alive? Or was it the dragon? That didn't make sense. It seemed identical to all the others the artist had crafted.

Moving to the window, he pushed aside the venetian blind and scanned the street. Bettnor had vanished. The whole business was infuriating. Maybe he should follow his original plans and go to Mexico, lie on a beach and forget all this. But that probably wouldn't work. Whatever someone thought he knew now, they'd still be sure he knew it when he got back.

And if his company was involved, he wanted to know it.

He mulled over Bettnor's last words. *Keep Malinche on a short rein.* Someone had already tried to harm her. Could he just walk away and leave her to face things alone? Or was she herself involved in this up to her pretty little neck?

A picture flashed through his mind. Malinche gazing up at him, her expression betraying her fear. There was more danger here than Carl Bettnor represented. He'd never had any trouble putting his feelings for a woman in the background. What made Malinche different? Especially when he knew she was the kind of woman who would never fit into his life? Bettnor was after something, possibly the dragon. And Brian had stupidly given it to Malinche. He might have placed her in more danger than she was in already.

He glanced at his watch, and grabbed his jacket from a peg in the foyer. If Bettnor was as thorough as he seemed to be, he might be heading for Malinche's apartment right now.

MALINCHE LISTENED to the strident ringing at the other end of the line, and sighed with relief when her father's voice boomed into the phone. "Hello?"

"Dad. I'm glad I caught you at home." Just hearing his voice made her feel less vulnerable. How could she be so ambivalent about Buck? She wanted autonomy, freedom, but he was the one she always called when she was in trouble.

"Is something wrong, angel?"

"You always could see right through me. I do have something to ask you. But I miss you, too," she insisted.

"Then come on home where you belong."

Malinche sighed. Her desire to find her roots, stand on her own two feet was a running argument between them. She knew her father didn't understand. He had ordered her not to come to Alaska, puzzled by her desire to delve back into her history, and she had defied him for perhaps the first time. There was no reason to resume the old argument.

"Dad, I've been thinking of Dimitri. I'm sure now he was murdered. You said that you were told that both he and his mother died during World War II. Just what were you told? And my mother? What really happened to her?"

Buck's voice came choked and husky over the line. "Just as I told you, sweetheart, she died when you were born. Your birth was hard. She was in her late thirties. Perhaps too old." His voice trailed away, then strengthened. "As to Marie and—my son—you remember hearing about the detention camp at Ward Cove, don't you?"

"Yes." She knew a little about it. At about the time the Japanese were involved at Midway, they attacked the Aleutian Islands. About 1400 Aleuts were living there, and to protect them the United States interned them at Ward Cove—a case of taking them from the frying pan to the fire.

"Marie and Dimitri were taken there. Your mother was there too, for a short time. She was a child. Twelve or thirteen. No wonder she wouldn't talk about it—it must have been hell. I only learned later how bad it was," Buck continued. "No heat, no food—while the fiercest battle of the war was waged on the Aleutians, the Aleuts were forgotten. When the war was over, over half the Aleuts were dead. I thought Marie—and my son—were among them."

"Marie may have died, but Dimitri didn't. I've got to help—"

"You shouldn't be worrying about it," Buck said. "Dimitri lived up there for years. He's bound to have friends who will do whatever is necessary."

"He was your son. My brother." The statement was an accusation.

"Yes. And if I'd have known that while he was alive, it would have been different. But it's in the past, Malinche."

She hung up, glad she hadn't told Buck about the threats to her life. He'd have been on the next plane to Alaska.

The sound of footsteps running upstairs alerted her. Apprehension fluttered along her spine. She held very still, every cell listening.

She peered through the window just in time to see Brian reaching for the bell.

Her heart gave a glad leap and she threw open the door, a smile on her face. "Didn't I just say good-night to you?"

He looked like a thundercloud ready to shoot a bolt

of lightning her way. "Do you always open your door without knowing who's out there?"

She lifted her chin. "I knew it was you. Besides, who appointed you my guardian?"

He moved past her, his sharp gray gaze moving quickly around the room. "Are you alone?"

"I'm not hiding a man in my closet, if that's what you mean."

"Sorry." He didn't look in the least sorry. He walked into the kitchen, then into her bedroom. She heard the door to the bedroom open and close before he finally came back into the living room.

Exasperation colored her voice. "Brian, what's going on? You left a couple of hours ago, saying you'd check a few things. I got the impression I wasn't at the top of your priorities. Now you come charging back, search my apartment and won't even tell me why."

He gave her a slow smile, a smile that turned her knees to jelly. She tried to ignore the tingle that ran along her arms, the shiver down her spine. Still, that wasn't reason enough to let him off the hook.

"Well?"

"I just wanted to make sure no one was here."

"And if someone was, what's it to you?"

He grinned then, a maddening grin. "Oh, I'm not worried about your love life. But I just had a very determined visitor, and I thought he might have come here. Believe me, he wasn't the kind I wanted hiding out with a gun pointed at me."

She stared back at him. "You came back because you were worried about me?"

"I know—you can take care of yourself."

He sprawled in a chair, his fingers laced together behind his head, and regarded her through smoky, hooded eyes. Their gazes met, held. A slow, warm current flowed through her, heating her blood, flooding her chest, coalescing in a point deep in her abdomen. She wanted him closer....

Her cheeks flushed. She was almost sure he knew exactly what she was thinking. She needed to break the connection, but should she slap his face or throw herself into his arms?

Neither, of course. She was reading too much into the moment. He was a healthy, sexy man, and he'd proven he was a take-charge kind. And he had some explaining to do. Was it just a coincidence that he, an employee of a company that had every reason to wish Dimitri out of the way, had been the one to find him?

She forced her gaze away from his. "Someone came to your apartment? What did they want?"

He shrugged. "To make very sure that questions about Dimitri stop. I thought I'd find out why."

"Does that mean you'll help me?"

He answered her question with one of his own. "Do you know Carl Bettnor?"

"Bettnor?" She shook her head. "No. Should I?"

"He certainly knows about you, and the questions you've been asking." He paused. She felt he was judging her, weighing every word she said. "Have you ever been involved with the CIA?"

"Of course not!"

"Don't look so indignant. It wouldn't be the first time they've used a beautiful woman. But I truly don't see how you'd fit. Anyway, Bettnor hinted that Dimitri was a threat to the government. Would you know anything about that?"

"Dimitri a spy?" She broke off. What did she really know about her brother? "I don't think it's likely," she said slowly. "From everything I've heard he was only interested in art."

"We seem to have a mystery here," Brian said. "Was Dimitri an artist, devoted only to his craft, or was he up to his neck in intrigue? I think I'd better find out."

"You mean *we*. I'm involved in this, don't forget."

"Oh, I don't forget that." Was there a double meaning in his words. "Anyway, no. It's too dangerous."

"Forget it! I won't be pushed aside."

He let it go, but she knew the argument wasn't over.

"There's one thing I'm sure of," Brian said. "People get murdered for a reason. Dimitri was either doing something or knew something that threatened someone. So the thing to do is find out who that someone was. I'll backtrack, talk to his friends, trace his movements all the way back to the time he was born if I have to. Do you know where he lived recently?"

He was ignoring everything she'd just said. "I'm not sure he had a permanent home," she replied icily. "But he had a studio and friends in Barrow. And you're not going there without me. I'll follow you if I have to." She'd had enough of being ordered around, treated like a child.

Brian hesitated, obviously mulling something over in his mind. "If you go with me, you're exposing yourself to danger. But you don't seem to be too safe here, either. All right. But don't slow me down. And remember, it's going to be tough. I'm not sure you can handle it."

"Don't worry about me," she said coldly. "But you'd better go home and get some sleep. We can start early in the morning—"

"I'm not going home."

Her eyes widened. "We can't start for Barrow right now—"

"I mean I'm spending the night here. You're not safe alone."

"Of course I'll be safe. I'll lock the door. Just because we're going to be together for a while doesn't mean you're going to be paid by—"

"Paid?" His voice was dangerously low. "Relax. I have no designs on your body."

She blushed furiously. Why had she jumped to such a conclusion? Because she had been thinking in those terms herself, wondering what he would be like?

"I appreciate the thought, but I'm afraid you can't stay," she muttered. "I have only one bed."

Brian's eyes went to the slim Edwardian couch. "That'll do. My bedroll's in the Jeep. I'll bring it in."

Malinche spent the short time he was gone desperately thinking of a way to dissuade him. It was all the more difficult because she was torn between fear of being alone and of Brian's being too close for comfort. Certainly all this macho protectiveness wasn't necessary. It was just the kind of man he was. The kind she didn't want.

But someone *had* been watching her apartment. Someone who might have different designs on her than the one's Brian said he *didn't* have.

He could deny it, but every feminine nerve ending told her Brian wasn't immune to this raging sexual awareness that had her trembling when he so much as looked at her.

Brian came through the door, his sleeping bag over his shoulder, his backpack on his arm.

"Looks like you came prepared," she said dryly.

"Always. That's the secret to survival in Alaska, as anyone but a *Cheechako* would know."

"*Cheechako?* You're referring to me?"

"*Cheechako,* newcomer, someone who never spent a winter up here. I'd say you qualify."

"I'd say you don't know what you're talking about. Remember, I spent the first few years of my life in an Indian village."

"But you forget quickly when the living is soft. How long since you've eaten muktuk?" he said, referring to the whale fat with skin attached which the Eskimos considered a delicacy.

"Probably about the last time you did."

"You've got me there," he said, grinning. "Still, you look like you belong in the lower forty-eight. Designer jeans, silk brocade—not a fingernail broken."

"And you can tell all about me just by looking at me?"

His eyes darkened. "I can tell a lot."

She sighed. "If you know where I belong, you're ahead of me."

The silence stretched between them, full of possibilities neither would acknowledge. Finally Malinche spoke.

"If there's nothing you need, I'll go on to bed." She gave him a wry smile. "I didn't realize it was so late. This constant daylight always makes it seem like the middle of the afternoon."

She took her time in the bathroom, smoothing fragrant lotion over her skin and inhaling the faint scent of jasmine. She had always loved that fragrance. It reminded her of balmy nights by a warm ocean, of a tropical moon in a black velvet sky....

What was she doing here at the frigid top of the

world, where the wind brought the biting scent of gla-
cier ice?

And especially what was she doing here with a dev-
astatingly attractive and sexy man on the other side of
the door? A man whom she sensed could show her all
the things she had been missing in relationships. At a
cost, of course. Of her autonomy.

She had long known there was an emptiness at her
core. An aching void she had to fill herself. She had
nothing to give until she solved her own dilemma. She
had come to Alaska looking for a way to unite the two
warring parts of herself.

She knew what she wanted in a man. She sensed in
herself a great passion, a deep capacity to love, and she
wanted the same capacity in a man. But she wanted
him to treat her as an equal, trust her judgment. The
man on the other side of the door wasn't like that.
There was no possibility of anything but physical passion between them.

With long, languorous strokes, she brushed her hair
until it flowed like a dark river along her cheek and
rested on her shoulders like the soft caress of a lover.
Removing a silk robe from a hook, she tightened it
around her waist and moved down the hall to her bedroom, acutely aware of Brian's presence.

"Bathroom's free," she called, and then shut her
door.

BRIAN STOOD in front of the lighted mirror, ruefully
rubbing the stubble on his chin and inhaling the light
fragrance of jasmine. The scent suited her—subtly
mysterious, lush, carrying a haunting hint of possibilities. What was stopping him? He had seen and rec-

ognized the heated look in her eyes, the yearning of a woman for physical love.

She wanted him. As much as he wanted her. The thought of her silky skin touched only by smooth sheets seemed a waste of womanhood. With any other woman, he wouldn't have hesitated.

Perversely, the very strength of his desire kept him decorously on his own side of the door. The urgency that sparked between them could easily turn into a conflagration—and that could get out of hand. Brian had no intention of being out of control.

He liked his life as it was. Oh, he thought about marrying someday, but it would be to a woman wise to the North who could handle hardship and loneliness. Malinche was too weak, soft from affluent living. He wondered how long she could keep up the pace he planned to set without collapsing and calling for Daddy.

He fervently wished he weren't mixed up in this, but Bettnor's visit had further convinced him he had no choice. He couldn't drop it. He wasn't going to tell Malinche about his own close calls, the threats to his life. He had nothing but her word about anything—that Dimitri was her brother, that she didn't know a lot more than she was telling.

He didn't know anything about her but what she had told him.

And what he saw of her. He caught his breath.

With the scent of her perfume still floating tantalizingly around him, invading every pore, every nerve, he rolled out his sleeping bag on the floor and shucked off his jeans and shirt. Wearing only his Jockey shorts, he slipped into the warm, down-filled bag.

He had decided against the couch. He suspected it's

fragile contours might not hold up to the tossing and turning he fully expected to do.

It was going to be a long, painful night. And he doubted that the next week or two would be much better.

Chapter Four

Brian pulled the Jeep into the parking lot near the lake where he kept his plane. As they rolled to a stop, Malinche jumped out and hoisted her bag from the vehicle.

Brian lifted an eyebrow. She was making a point. She'd probably never carried her own bag in her life. She would find soon enough that this trip was going to involve more hardship than lifting a small bag. He tried to ignore the tightness in his chest as he watched the way her jeans clung to her adorable backside. He had to make sure his emotions weren't also involved.

"What did you do with the dragon?" he asked, lifting out his own bag.

She turned and fingered a delicate gold chain around her neck. "It's here. I didn't want to leave it in my apartment. I think someone wants this very much."

"I suggest you keep your shirt buttoned, then."

"I'm not a fool. It's safe here."

"Maybe. I think you should throw it away."

"I appreciate everything you're doing, Brian. But you can't tell me what to do."

Brian shrugged and strode after her along the pier. If this was going to become a battle of wills, he would regret allowing her to come along more than he already did.

He slung his bag into the plane and stood back, grinning, while she tossed hers after it. "You've got a pretty good swing," he said, and was rewarded by a brilliant smile. Maybe things wouldn't be so bad after all.

"Hey, Brian!"

Startled, Brian turned toward the voice. A canoe slid across the lake and nudged the pier, and a short, stocky man carrying a fishing pole lumbered up onto the pier. He would have looked more at home in a business suit than the new flannel shirt and dungarees he wore.

"Joe. What are you doing here?" Brian caught the line from the canoe and wrapped it around a pole. "I didn't know you were a fisherman."

"You know you can't be an Alaskan and not fish," Joe said. "They'd run you out of the state." He glanced at Malinche, but spoke to Brian. "I'm surprised to see you here, pal. I thought you'd be heading for Mexico, but now I see the attraction in hanging around."

"Malinche, this is my boss, Joe Pasco." As Malinche held out her hand, Brian gazed thoughtfully at Joe. He'd known the man a long time, and had never suspected he would be up at dawn casting into a lake. Perhaps he didn't know the man as well as he thought he did.

"Where are you headed, Brian?" Joe asked. "I thought you just got back from your rustic hideaway."

"You know me—I love the wilderness," Brian replied.

"I think I'd like it better myself with the right company." Pasco smiled at Malinche. "Any place I can get in touch with you in case something comes up?"

There was no reason not to tell Pasco their destination. Joe was a friend; he often checked Brian's house while he was gone. Come to think of it, he'd had plenty of opportunity to search it, too.

"We'll be going from place to place," Brian said. "Good luck with your fishing."

Joe sketched a salute, and stood on the pier as the two entered the plane and taxied out over the water. When they lifted off Joe was still there, staring after them.

"Your boss seems very interested in our trip," Malinche remarked, as they gained altitude and left the bowl of Anchorage behind them. "Do you suppose he followed us to the lake?"

Brian shrugged. "His being there was just a coincidence. Why would he follow us?"

"You and I both know that Universal Oil wasn't happy with Dimitri's activities. Maybe they don't want us snooping around."

"Forget it. My employers may play hardball sometimes, but they aren't murderers. Besides, it wouldn't be necessary. Dimitri couldn't have been that effective—he obviously wasn't getting far with convincing the other Natives. Universal Oil could get permission to drill without doing away with Dimitri."

Silence stretched between them. Malinche gazed down at the mountains thrusting jagged peaks toward the tiny plane as though they would like to tear it from the skies. Peak after snowy peak interspersed with stands of conifers, looking from this distance like a dark blanket wrapped around the mountains' feet. A fierce and rugged land, alien to her after her life in the lower forty-eight. What was she doing here? Why did she have such an obsessive need to find her roots?

And why was she so achingly aware of this man beside her? She sneaked a look at his profile, and found it hard to breathe. No question about where he belonged. If ever a man fit perfectly with his environment, it was he. He sat relaxed and confident, flying this fragile craft across a wilderness. So sure about this, and that he knew what was best for everyone.

Had he known Pasco was going to see them off? Had some signal passed between them? She had known him such a short time, and she couldn't afford to let her guard down. Still, she had an unreasonable feeling that he could look into her heart. She had wondered last night if he would check her door, and had been unreasonably disappointed that he had not.

She gave up soul-searching and settled in for the long flight to Barrow.

Barrow, although she had seen pictures, was still a surprise. A bleak, flat town of shanties fronted with snowmobiles and dogs, it was like neither the village she had been born in nor the sophistication of Anchorage.

The taxi at the airport was a beat-up Jeep driven by a Native who said his name was George.

George. Wasn't that the name of Dimitri's friend, the one who had sent her the package? Still, the name wasn't unusual. She'd ask him. Short and squat, with the broad face of an Eskimo, George had a cheery smile that gave her confidence. Not so the road. Snow and ice still lingered here, so near the Pole, and Malinche held her breath as they skidded on an icy stretch. George, seemingly unconcerned, dodged a pothole and shouted over the roar of the noisy engine.

"Where are you staying?" he asked over the engine noise.

"Not sure," Brian shouted back. "Did you know Dimitri Stanislof?"

George became suddenly very attentive to the road. Perhaps he hadn't understood.

"We're looking for someone who knew Dimitri Stanislof," Malinche echoed. "He was a famous artist who had a studio here."

George, the cheery smile gone, pulled to the side of the road and cut the engine. "Maybe. Who wants to know?"

A moment ago George's face had been open and friendly. Now it was as enigmatic as the frozen tundra itself.

"I'm his sister. Malinche Adams. This is Brian Kennedy."

He stared at her so long she thought he wasn't going to respond at all. "Malinche Adams," he finally said. "His sister? You're the one I sent the package to. You know he's dead."

Malinche's breath caught in her throat. This was indeed the George who had sent her the package and Dimitri's letter. His friend. She took a deep breath.

"That's why we're here, to find out why he died. Can you tell us anything that might help find who killed him?"

George's expression was blanker than before. "I can't tell you anything."

"Perhaps if we could see his studio?" Brian interjected. "He may have left a clue of some kind."

Again George hesitated, then made up his mind. "I guess it can't hurt. I doubt you'll find anything. I already looked through it. I have the key. You can stay there, if you like.''

"You must have known him very well," Malinche ventured.

"As well as anyone, I guess. No one knew him well." George turned the key in the ignition, and pulled back into the street.

A few minutes later, with a screech of tires, he pulled up in front of a shanty, and leaped to the ground. "Bring your stuff. I'll open the door."

Malinche shivered. A chilly wind blew unhindered over the flat landscape, a landscape whose monotony was broken only by a few hillocks of scrawny vegetation. Such openness made her feel vulnerable, uneasy.

George caught her glance and a flash of amusement lit his black eyes. "He liked his privacy." He pushed open the door and stood aside as Malinche and Brian entered the small room.

Dimitri's essence met her, engulfed her. She caught her breath, and tears stung her eyes. Her late brother's studio was vibrant, glowing, filled with his work. How much she had missed by not knowing him.

She moved about, reverently touching each object. Tanned walrus hides covered the plank floor. A baleen sculpture, with musk oxen and wolves boldly etched, crowned the one small window. Bears, seals, eagles, covered most of the other spaces, each lovingly carved from walrus tusks.

And there, in a place of honor on a hand-carved chest, rested a dozen dragons, carved from ivory and jade, the writhing forms ranging from half an inch to a full twelve inches in size, his only departure from traditional Native art.

Brian followed Malinche around the room. "I see what you meant. He was a great artist."

"The best," George agreed.

"I almost feel as if he's still here," Malinche said softly. "Or his spirit." She touched the tip of her finger to a large ivory bear. The animal felt warm, alive to her touch. Hatred for his killer burst inside her. She burned, she lusted, to find out who had stopped this wonderfully creative artist in the midst of his work. Who had robbed her of her birthright?

"Did you know him well?" Malinche asked softly.

"As well as anyone, I guess, but he was a loner. He didn't tell me much about his past life. I learned he'd been at Ward Cove when he was just a child. I never knew for sure what he did when he got out of there, or where he lived until he came here. By that time he was getting a small reputation as an artist."

Ward Cove. The name sent shivers down her back. Her mother had been in Ward Cove, too. She shook off the thought.

"Do you want to stay here for the night?" George broke into her thoughts. "I don't know what you're looking for, but if it will help find Dimitri's killer—"

"Then you agree he was murdered?" Malinche spun toward him.

"I don't see what else it could have been. People say he wandered out in the snow and froze to death, but he wouldn't do that."

"He didn't. We found out he was stabbed," Brian said tersely.

"Expected so." George's face was expressionless. "But you won't find anything here to prove it. I've looked." He turned to go. "There's a café down the road, but I don't think Dimitri would mind if you used his supplies. He won't be needing them. I'll stop by in the morning.'' With a wave of his hand, he went out the door, and in a moment, she heard the roar of the Jeep's motor.

Malinche lifted the largest of the jade dragons from the chest. At first glance, they all looked slightly different, but on closer examination, she saw they were all the same type—a heraldic dragon, sinewy tail coiled around four-clawed legs, a ridge of sharp spines stretching from the spiked nose to the forked tail. Fiery, malignant eyes, a barbed tongue protruding from an open mouth. Their ferocity made her shudder.

It seemed incongruous that Dimitri, with his gentle seals and bears and eagles, should carve this ferocious fantasy.

She replaced it on the chest, keenly aware, as always, of Brian's presence. "What do you think of George? Does he know more than he's telling?"

"I doubt it," Brian said. "He wouldn't have left us here alone if he had anything to hide."

"I suppose you're right." She smiled, looking up into his eyes, eyes that could change from hard steel to warm soft clouds in an instant. Eyes that she could drown in. It was a bad move. His eyes held her, caressed her, and she suspected it had occurred to him, as it had to her, that they would be spending the night alone together.

"We'd better start looking," she said, hoping her tremulous voice wouldn't betray her thoughts.

Two hours later she leaned on the file cabinet in the tiny alcove, so close to Brian that with only a shift in weight she would touch him. In spite of the distraction of his nearness, she knew they had searched thoroughly. Nothing.

She shoved a file folder back in an open drawer, and sighed. "He sure was involved in a lot of things, but I don't see how any of it relates to his death."

"Me, either." Brian scanned a letter Dimitri had received from the secretary of a Native corporation. "We're just confirming what we knew. He stirred up a lot of people—but none of them seem likely to have killed him."

"What about the CIA agent you said entered your apartment? Could Dimitri really have been a spy?"

"There's nothing here to confirm it." He dropped the letter on top of the file cabinet, then swore as it slipped down behind it. He reached down to retrieve it, and pulled out the letter and another envelope along with it. "What's this?"

Malinche's quick surge of hope melted into disappointment. "It's just an empty envelope."

"But it's from the Department of the Army in Washington. Why would the army be writing to him?"

"If he were a spy? A double agent?"

"Then I'd expect he'd be dealing with the CIA, not the army. Maybe George can tell us more about it in the morning."

He glanced at Malinche, and felt such a surge of desire that he forgot about the envelope. She looked so tired, so fragile, that it was all he could do to stop himself from crossing the few inches between them and taking her in his arms, cradling her head against his chest. He wanted to kiss the top of her head where the whiteness of the part showed between the dark wings of her hair, kiss the back of her neck, the soft hollow at her throat....

And that was dangerous. He already knew she was fragile, unfit for the hardships of his life. She brought out the need to protect and shield, making him forget that in the end it would be he who needed the protection. He'd get his mind off her. He didn't want to spend tonight tossing as he had last night. He wasn't going to let his mind wander to her soft full lips, or dream about her silky skin beneath his hands.

"Good luck," he murmured to himself, suspecting it was already too late. "Maybe we'd better look around for some food," he said aloud.

"You're right. I'm hungry. Let's see what we can find."

The cupboard yielded several cans of beans, sardines, peaches, and an unopened can of coffee. Brian groaned.

"Don't be such a sissy." Malinche laughed, a deep throaty laugh that sent shivers all through Brian. "Aren't you the man who could eat muktuk?"

"I was lying."

Malinche bent to pick up a pan, her breasts pushing against her sweater, and heat rushed to his face. Malinche was all wrong for him, and he still didn't quite trust her. Although George had confirmed that Dimitri had believed her to be his sister. Maybe she was telling the truth. But truth or not, she didn't belong in his world.

He watched her spoon the beans into a saucepan, her slender body moving gracefully, her sooty eyelashes starkly outlined against her clear skin. A strand of hair had escaped the braid and fell over her ivory cheekbone. Absently, she reached up and pushed it behind her ear. The movement went straight to Brian's heart. Mesmerized, he watched her. A faint beading of moisture shone above her upper lip. Her full lips parted slightly…

He didn't know how he got there. He didn't make a conscious plan, but suddenly his hand was on the back of her neck, his mouth seeking hers. She was warm and pliant in his arms, her soft breath a faint caress on his skin.

She didn't resist. In fact, she melded herself against him, her breasts pressing insistently against his chest. His loins caught fire, his embrace tightened. He wanted her, wanted to impress himself on every part of her. He deepened his kiss, insistent, demanding, and felt fiery exultation as she opened her lips to him.

The scent of jasmine engulfed him, and something more—the sweet essence of her femininity welcomed him. For an endless minute he clung to her, desire building to a crescendo.

With an obvious effort, she pulled away, her whisper sounding husky and reluctant in his ears. "I—Brian—no."

Immediately, he released her. The swift sense of loss was so keen he had to exert every ounce of willpower not to pull her to him again. "I'm sorry. I didn't mean to take advantage…" *What had he meant to do, then?* he thought, cursing his weakness. The truth was, he hadn't thought at all. She was just there, irresistible, calling to the male in him.

"You didn't take advantage," she whispered, still breathless, clutching at the chair back to regain her composure. "But it mustn't happen again."

His gaze followed hers to the single bed, and he sighed. "I know. I just forgot myself for a minute." He turned as though pursued by demons and rushed out the door. In a few minutes he was back, bringing his sleeping bag with him. He spread it on the floor on the far side of the room.

Later, although the oil stove heated the room, Malinche felt cold as she lay in her narrow bed. She admitted she wanted Brian's arms around her, his legs intertwined with hers. She wanted to rest her face against the moist, hard muscles of his chest, smell the masculine aroma that would rise from his heated skin. And she had to fight her body's demand. It could only be sexual attraction; Brian wasn't the kind of man she could commit to for life. He was a hard masculine force who would always threaten her desire for autonomy, her need to be an equal. He treated her with a kind of patronizing kindness that let her know what he thought of her.

She listened for his breathing. He was awake, too, perhaps having as hard a time as she at forgetting the dizzying moment of passion between them. When sleep finally came, it was broken with dreams of a strong, controlling man pushing her toward a precipice.

"WHAT IS IT?" Brian mumbled, fighting up out of the sleep that had finally come to him.

"There! Don't you hear it?"

The panic in her voice jarred him wide awake. He stilled his breathing, straining to hear. There *was* something—a whisper of stealthy footsteps, the creak of leather on frozen sod.

He grabbed his Smith & Wesson revolver from beneath his bag and crept to the door, flinging it open.

The sharp crack of a pistol split the arctic silence. A bullet slammed into the doorjamb. He sprang back.

"Stay down, Malinche!"

He kicked the door shut and inched to the window and peered out, careful to keep out of the line of vision of whoever was outside. At this time of year, above the arctic circle, the sun never set, and daylight illuminated the landscape. He saw no one, but the attacker could be behind a hillock. Or he might have taken one shot and ran like hell.

He cracked the window and shot into the air. The echo reverberated, but there was no other sound.

Malinche clutched his arm, her eyes on the weapon in his hand. "I didn't know you had a gun with you."

"You were supposed to stay down! You'd better learn to follow orders if you want to survive! And you didn't think I'd be dumb enough to come unarmed looking for a killer?"

"But you shot in the air."

"Because I don't know where he is. I hope that shot warned him off. He'll know we're not defenseless."

She was holding him firmly around the waist. It felt good. Too good. He knew the tendency, when in danger, to search for safety, for comfort, in someone's arms. That was all her embrace meant.

Gently, he guided Malinche back to the bed and convinced her to lie down. With a sigh, she relaxed against the pillow, her hair dark against the pale material, her body soft and yielding. If he were a different kind of man he would take advantage of her dependency, her need for comfort. Even knowing she would hate him for it, almost as much as he would hate himself, it still took all his willpower not to join her.

And he couldn't afford a distraction, not with a killer loose. This was not the time to be caught with his pants down.

Chapter Five

Malinche awoke to the aroma of fresh-brewed coffee, and stifled the impulse to pull the comforter up over her head. Last night's attack had replayed in her mind until she had thought she would never get to sleep. For hours she had lain awake, heart pounding, listening for footsteps outside the door.

It was annoying to hear Brian's deep, even breathing. Had the man no sensitivity at all? Eventually, though, she had fallen into a druggedlike sleep.

Turning her head, she saw Brian's back, watched as he reached into the cupboard for mugs. Her heart skipped a beat. The sight chased away any remnants of sleep. In his faded jeans and chamois shirt, his thick blond hair tousled from sleep, he looked lean and powerful, a man in control of his environment.

He was a puzzle. The kiss they had shared still pulsed in her blood. It was difficult to think he had anything to hide. But why had he refused to help her and then changed his mind so quickly? What wasn't he telling her?

She guessed she should ask him this question. But he was helping her, and if he had anything to hide, he certainly wasn't likely to tell her.

"Time to wake up, sleepyhead."

"I'm awake. Barely." She had slept in her silk long johns. Now she swung her legs over the side of the bed, brushed her hair from her eyes, and reached for the coffee.

"It's nine o'clock. After last night's drama, I thought you'd better sleep a little."

She fumbled for her cup, her hand brushing his. Calling on willpower he didn't know he had, Brian didn't flinch, although her touch traveled up his arm like warm honey. God, she was beautiful, rising from sleep like Aphrodite from the waves.

He caught his breath. Desire burned all along his veins. How much longer could he go on pretending this was nothing but physical need? He no longer thought she was involved with the CIA, but he was quite sure she didn't belong in his world. He'd heard of her father, Buck Adams. When things got tough, she would run to Daddy.

But knowing that didn't help him now. She lifted worried eyes to him, sending shivers all along his spine. It would be easy to forget that he must keep his distance.

"Brian—who shot at us last night?"

"Could have been anyone. Probably trying to scare us."

"Well, he succeeded."

He walked to the door, ostensibly to examine the bullet hole, but in reality to give himself time to think. He had to get Malinche out of this situation, send her home to Seattle, while he continued to investigate. There was a phantom out there, determined to stop them, and he could handle that much better without having her around to worry about. Although she was holding up better than he had thought she would.

"Get dressed," he said abruptly. "I'll check outside."

He didn't expect to find anything, and he didn't. In the tundra, footsteps would never show up. The scant vegetation appeared undisturbed. The shooter could have walked from one of the houses, visible several hundred yards away, or he could have parked a vehicle down the road. One thing was sure—he was still out there.

He stiffened at the sound of a motor, then relaxed as he recognized George's battered Jeep.

"Got any coffee?" George pulled up, splashing gravel, and jumped out beside him.

"Sure. Come inside."

At the sound of the door opening, Malinche glanced up from the frying pan in which hash sizzled enticingly. In jeans, a soft mauve turtleneck sweater and Italian leather boots, she looked as though she'd be right at home in Seattle. Not here.

"Hi, guys. How about breakfast?"

"Wow. If that tastes as good as it smells, you could have a permanent job." Brian immediately regretted his words. It was a casual remark, but he didn't even want to joke about permanency where Malinche was concerned.

George gulped the hot strong coffee. His face wrinkled with perplexity when Brian told him about their nighttime visitor.

"No idea who it could have been," he said, rubbing his chin with a square, strong hand. "This is a small town…people sometimes get a little too much to drink and cause a little trouble, but there's no reason a local would shoot up the place.''

"Have any strangers been around recently?"

"Some. Always are in the summer. Early June is our busiest time. I hang out at the airport picking up a few bucks driving people to the hotel, but I don't see everybody. Lots of them have convertible planes like yours—they can land most anyplace.''

That avenue led nowhere. Brian pulled the empty envelope from his pocket. "Do you know anything about this?''

"An empty envelope?''

"It's from the Department of the Army in Washington. Why would Dimitri have a letter from them?''

"He was writing to the army about something,'' George said slowly. "All winter he seemed distracted, upset. He wouldn't say much, but he seemed to be thinking a lot about the time he spent at Ward Cove. He was just a kid, you know, and I gathered it was pretty bad. His mother died there. He seemed more obsessed than ever with dragons. What's the date on that letter?''

Brian handed him the envelope, and George scanned the date. "He left for Kotzebue a couple of days after he got that letter. He was real excited about something, but he wouldn't tell me what. Just said he was getting close, and he had to see somebody there.'' He glanced at Malinche. "And if he didn't come back, I was to send you that package.''

"He knew he was in danger, then. Why would he go to Kotzebue?''

"No idea. Every year since the cold war ended the Eskimos from here and Siberia have been meeting along the coast like they used to do. You know—relatives seeing each other, old friends meeting. It's a good place for gossip. This year the gathering was near Kotzebue.''

And a good place to pass information if you're a spy. ''I found his body midway between Kotzebue and Prudhoe Bay,'' Brian said. ''I guess Kotzebue is the next stop.''

Malinche, who had already tidied up the dishes, was packing her bag. Brian frowned. She didn't realize what she was getting into. Nothing in her experience had prepared her for the kind of danger they might face.

''I want you to go back to Seattle,'' he said sternly. ''A shuttle leaves for Anchorage today. I'll go on to Kotzebue—''

Her mutinous look stopped him in the middle of the sentence. Okay, so she wouldn't listen to reason. Stubborn. Malinche continued her silence as she got in the Jeep and they traversed the bumpy road to the airport.

Several minutes later George pulled his Jeep up beside Brian's Cessna. ''I gassed up for you yesterday in case you wanted to leave in a hurry. It's a long drag to Kotzebue.''

''Well...thanks,'' Brian said uneasily. George's action was only one of friendly help, and Brian convinced himself he was getting too suspicious of everyone. He peeled some bills from his pocket and handed them to George. ''This should take care of everything.''

George pocketed the money. ''Sure you've got enough of everything? You can reach me on the radio if you have any trouble.''

''I'm not a *Cheechako*,'' Brian said dryly. ''I'm prepared for emergencies. Thanks for everything.'' Brian walked slowly around the plane. Everything seemed in order.

A few minutes later the plane lifted smoothly from the ground and Brian pointed it toward Kotzebue.

When they reached cruising altitude, Malinche leaned back and ran her hands through her long hair. She hadn't braided it this morning, and it felt sensuous on her skin, caressing the back of her neck—as Brian's hand had done so recently. Disconcerting how the feel of his touch still lingered.

"George seemed strange," she said slowly, glancing down at the endless rolling tundra cut here and there by small rivulets. "Do you suppose he's not telling us everything he knows?"

"Who ever is?" Brian retorted.

They were silent, as below them the tundra stretched forever. Here and there washes of color indicated the brief arctic summer had finally arrived.

"It seems such an inhospitable land," Malinche said softly. "To think my ancestors actually lived here, killed game, raised families—such a primitive life…" Her voice trailed away.

"Some of your ancestors lived here," Brian retorted. "The rest were in Europe, busy hacking up enemies with broadaxes, painting themselves blue before they went into battle."

She smiled. "I get your point. My Scotch-Irish side could be primitive, too. Sometimes I wonder where I fit in all this—what my world really is."

"Your world is what you make it. Forget about the past. The present is all you have."

"Is that what you do, live in the present? Don't you ever think of the future, of having a family?"

"I never think much about it."

She glanced at his rock-hard profile. He was so sure of himself, so confident of his place in the world, while she was constantly searching for something she might not recognize even if she found it.

Since leaving Barrow they had not seen one human habitation. They'd flown over a herd of caribou and a herd of musk ox, but the humans who had been here once had left no trace. She felt uneasy, lonely, vulnerable in the fragile plane. This was nothing compared with what her hunter ancestors had faced, following the animals across the Bering Strait into a harsh, unknown land, yet it took all her courage to merely fly above it.

Thinking of those long-ago people, she felt the tug of kinship, of continuity. Had some woman, her age perhaps, with children in tow, followed her man into this wilderness? Where one mishap would be the last? That was something she, shielded by civilization, would never know.

The drone of the engine, the monotonous vibration of the aircraft, made her drowsy. She felt nearly at peace, with Brian's competent hand on the wheel. Would it be so bad to be taken care of? Immediately she rejected the thought. That was what she was running from. "How much longer?"

"We're about halfway. Try to get a little more sleep."

"That's a good—" She broke off, alarmed by a slight sputter in the engine. "Is something wrong?"

"No—" Brian's expression belied the word, and she was instantly fully awake.

The engine coughed, and Brian pulled out the throttle to give it more fuel. Incredulous, he glanced at the gauge. It had shown full when they left Barrow, but for the last few minutes it had been dropping alarmingly. Now, impossibly, the needle rested on empty.

He repressed his surge of alarm, as he sought and rejected several alternatives. He didn't want to frighten Malinche, but things didn't look good. He had checked the plane himself before leaving Anchorage, and it was in perfect condition. Since then no one had been near it—

Except George. And anyone else who happened to be wandering around the airport while he slept. Yet everything had looked all right when he made his quick check.

The engine, after one last ineffectual sputter, quit entirely.

"Brian!" Malinche gazed at him with wide, frightened eyes. "What's the matter?"

"I have to take her down. Put your head down!"

Thank God she didn't scream or distract him with frantic questions. This plane could land on most anything—snow, water, land—when he put the wheels down, but without power it was going to be tricky.

He concentrated on the controls, using every bit of skill he possessed. There was no reason to pick a spot; one place looked about the same as another. "Here goes! Hang on!"

With a bump that jarred him down to the soles of his feet, they came to a crashing stop.

He sat there, not even bothering to brush the sweat from his face. They were upright, the plane was intact, but without gas it didn't make a great deal of difference.

"Are you all right?" He turned to Malinche, his chest tight with fear. If anything happened to her, it would be his fault.

She was slumped in her seat, her eyes scrunched shut. She opened them slowly and took a long, shaky breath. ''All right? I'm not dead, if that's what you mean. What happened?''

Relief flooded him. Thank God, she was safe, and it didn't appear she was going to have hysterics. ''You're not going to believe this—but we ran out of gas.'' He felt as shaky as she looked, but he could still make a joke.

''That old story. If you're expecting me to say I'll walk home, forget it!''

It was unreal, she thought. A moment ago she had been looking down on this barren landscape wondering how her ancient ancestors had felt and now here she was, stranded.

The silence, after the drone of the plane, was deafening. Oppressive. It awoke the atavistic fear of the unknown, and frightened her more than anything else. It reminded her that they were uncounted miles from any other humans, any possible help. They were alone in a bleak and unforgiving land.

Without conscious volition, she reached out to touch Brian. His hand closed over hers, bringing comfort and strength. ''What do we do now?'' she whispered.

''I don't know. But I better take a look at the plane.'' Reluctantly, he released her hand and swung from the plane. He knew where to look for trouble. The gas line. It didn't take long to find it. A tiny slit had been drilled in the line, and the vibration of the plane had widened it enough to let the gas pour out in a steady stream. Someone had sabotaged the plane. Someone had wanted them to plunge into the most isolated land in the state.

His mouth tightened. The same person who had sabotaged his Jeep. This confirmed that they were being followed.

Malinche had climbed down and stood beside him. "Can you fix it?" she asked.

"I can fix the cut—but I can't manufacture gas."

"Then we're stuck here," she said, shivering. "What will we do?"

"We have emergency supplies. And George said to radio him if we had trouble."

He knew the thought was in Malinche's mind as well as his. What if George was the reason they were here?

Brian stepped back into the plane and tried the radio. "Mayday, Mayday. We need assistance. Come in if you can hear me."

He flipped the switch, waited. Nothing.

He tried again, giving their location and requesting help. Still nothing. Finally he climbed back down to where Malinche waited. "Perhaps he heard us, but our receiver isn't working."

"Don't patronize me. We're stuck here."

He didn't deny it. They needed to find a shelter where they could build a fire. A search would eventually be mounted, but he had no idea how soon. And there was a lot of ground to search.

He hoisted a bag from the cargo hold and handed it to Malinche, then lifted another onto his shoulder. He also took his rifle from behind the seat of the plane.

"We've plenty of food and water," he said, trying to make his tone cheerful and confident. "I don't want to get far from the plane. Let's see if we can find a shelter nearby."

She nodded and shouldered the bag, but her glance around indicated how dubious she was. The land was mostly flat with an occasional rolling hill. Nothing—

no tree, no boulder, impeded the relentless onslaught of the wind.

Brian glanced at her face, momentarily distracted from the peril of their situation. He had expected she would look incongruous here in the wild, with her sleek down jacket and designer jeans, but somehow she didn't. And she wasn't complaining, although she must be cold. She was doing just fine, he thought grudgingly. Still, they needed a shelter where they could build a fire.

Their only hope of rescue was to stay fairly close to the plane. Besides, they couldn't get far on foot. He scanned the horizon, searching for anything—a mound, a ravine—that might shelter them from the wind. Malinche trudged beside him, now and again shifting the bag of supplies from one shoulder to the other. The weight was too much for her fragile frame. She couldn't keep this up for long. He should have insisted that she return to Seattle.

He thought he heard something, a far-off drone. He shook his head. It was only the wind in the scrub brush.

Then he saw something that brought a surge of optimism; he almost shouted aloud. Several hundred feet away, in the side of a slight elevation, a dark spot appeared. A cave! He hoped desperately it was large enough to shelter the two of them.

He hadn't noticed that the faint sound he'd heard had increased to a low drone. He gazed up at the sky.

Malinche halted, and slid the bag from her shoulder. "Look! Is that a plane?"

The dark speck in the sky became the definite silhouette of a plane. Brian waved his arms wildly. "Here we are!"

The plane, directly overhead now, dived toward them.

Brian dropped his arms, and his mouth opened in dismay. The sharp sounds coming from the plane sounded like rifle shots.

The plane came so close he thought it might crash before it leveled off, gained altitude, and prepared for another dive.

He looked at the cave, still a hundred feet away. "Run!"

Malinche didn't hesitate. She saw the opening and ran.

They reached it together and fell inside just as a hail of bullets from the diving plane spattered behind them.

Chapter Six

Malinche sprawled headlong into the dust. Pinned by Brian's arm across her shoulders, she lay there, unable to move, her heart pounding like a trip-hammer. In her mind's eye, she saw the rain of bullets tearing up bits of grass and turf outside the entrance. Every gasp of breath carried the fine dry silt of the cave's interior into her lungs.

Sputtering and choking, she squirmed from under his arm. Twisting her face to the side, she found herself staring directly into his eyes, only a few inches away. She managed a tiny gasp.

He grasped her arm. "Are you all right?"

She wanted to laugh or cry or scream—she didn't know which. Was she all right? Since coming to Alaska, she had been run down by an automobile, shot at by some crazy person, crash-landed in a plane in the middle of nowhere, and she was now lying flat on her stomach inside a dusty cave while someone circled above in a plane, shooting at her.

"I'm great," she muttered, wiping dust from her mouth with a shaking hand, "just great."

She rolled to her side and sat up, drawing her knees up toward her chest. Halfheartedly, she swiped at her jeans, trying to dislodge the dust, only to have it rise in a cloud to her face.

"Somehow, this wasn't what I had in mind when I wondered how my ancestors lived. I really don't need a direct experience."

He sat up, too, drawing his long legs in from the opening. He was as dusty as though he had just slid to home base. Dark streaks covered his forehead, his nose, ran down his jaw, emphasizing the startling gray of his eyes, the whiteness of his teeth when he grinned at her. Even now, when she was scared to death, he was too darn sexy for comfort.

Turning serious, he said, "The plane seemed to come from nowhere. It probably followed us the whole time."

"Is he still out there?"

Both she and Brian were silent, listening for the sound that would tell them the plane still circled above them. It came, an ominous, monotonous drone that vibrated all through her.

"He's still there," Brian whispered.

They waited several more minutes, listening to the plane circle above them like some huge, predatory insect.

"What if he lands?" Malinche whispered. She felt foolish immediately. Whoever was up there wouldn't hear them if she shouted, but she couldn't force herself to raise her voice.

"He won't," Brian said. "He must know I have a rifle, and a pistol. If he tried to get us here, I could pick him off from the entrance. It's a stalemate. We can't get out of here while he's above us, and he can't flush us out of this cave."

"How long will we have to stay here?"

"Not long. He'll run out of gas if he keeps this up. He obviously planned to shoot us on the ground, and our stumbling into this cave messed up his plans."

"I think this time he meant to do more than scare us," Malinche said, shivering.

"Yes," Brian agreed. "If he shot us out here on the open tundra he could count on wolves or other wild animals destroying the evidence. That is, if we were found at all." He rose to his feet, his head grazing the ceiling of the cave. "Let's check out this place— we may be here awhile."

Brian moved back into the darkness, and she followed closely, curious now that they were safe for the moment. She had supposed they had stumbled into a natural cavern, but the cave was obviously man-made, apparently the abode of the ancient hunters who had come this way.

The narrow entry, perhaps kept small for defensive purposes, widened into a round room with sloping walls shored up with the long bones of caribou. A minuscule amount of light filtered through the entry, sufficient for them to make out indentations in the wall, narrow benches where sleeping skins must once have been. A blackened spot in the middle of the floor still contained charcoal from an ancient fire. Smoke-encrusted walls and ceiling indicated the cave had been inhabited over a long period.

A glance at Brian's expression showed he shared her awe.

Malinche found her voice first. "It must have been here for hundreds of years."

"Perhaps thousands," Brian said. He stood in an attitude of listening, as though he expected long-dead voices to murmur and speak in their ancient tongue.

"Maybe this was made by the first people who crossed over from Asia. Think how it must have been. Can you feel the spirits of the people? I wonder if it was used only by hunters for shelter when they were away from the home village, or did entire families live here?"

Malinche nodded; she knew exactly how he felt, but she wouldn't have expected such sentiment from Brian. She knelt and picked up a piece of ivory that had been carved into a shaft with a hollow globe at the end. It made a rattling noise when she lifted it, exactly as a baby's rattle would. Perhaps some long-gone hunter had whiled away a winter here, carving walrus tusks.

"I think a family lived here," she said softly, almost afraid to break the ancient silence. "Or several. I wonder what happened to them, where they came from, where they went…"

"I don't know—but I sure thank them." Brian said. "We could have walked for miles and never found something like this. We were lucky."

"Yes, we were. He *must* be gone by now." Malinche moved toward the entrance to the cave. When she heard nothing she peered out. She saw only empty tundra, its brooding silence unbroken by the sound of the plane. Only the wind, relentless as time, moved the grasses in an unending sigh.

"Yeah, he's gone—for now," Brian said, coming to stand beside her.

"So, what do we do now? We can't just wait here for him to come back and finish us off."

Brian hated to say so, but there was really no other choice. They could never walk to safety, not with their unknown assailant unaccounted for. The probability was good that he would be waiting to gun them down. They had to stay where they were for the time being.

That only pushed their dilemma ahead a few days. True, here they had shelter from the wind. In fact, the cave would be quite cozy when he had a fire burning on the old hearth. The food and water would last a few days. After that he might be able to find some kind of game—an arctic hare or fox, perhaps. And there might be water close by. Even if the man in the plane came back again and again, Brian could probably manage quick forays outside.

But they couldn't stay here forever. Their only hope was that rescue would come. In the meantime, he had better keep Malinche busy and try to keep her mind off their situation. She'd done fine so far, but it was only a matter of time before she broke down. He felt her hand rest lightly on his arm, and turned to find her gazing up into his eyes.

"Brian," she said softly, "why did you finally decide to help me? You've gotten yourself into a lot of trouble on my account."

"Because you're so pretty?" he said lightly.

"Don't joke. Is there something you're not telling me?"

He frowned, and laid his hand lightly over hers. "Let's just say I had some things to resolve, too. Don't feel that you talked me into anything I didn't want to do."

She sighed. He obviously wasn't going to say anything else.

He turned away from her. "Let's get a fire going," he said cheerfully. "I'll gather some dry moss and you rummage around in that pack for matches. You might also unpack our supplies, so we can see how long they'll last."

Malinche watched him exit the cave, and then turned

to the task he had assigned her. He was trying to keep her occupied. He would know to the last pack of trail mix what supplies he had. Nonetheless, she was glad to have something to occupy her hands; her mind was racing like a rabbit trying to keep ahead of a grey-hound.

What had she started when she decided to find out who had killed her brother? It seemed naive now, her belief that she could discover what so many people were determined to cover up. This was no casual enemy, but a well-prepared, well-supplied one. She doubted that George had such a systematic mind. Who did her determination to find Dimitri's killer threaten? Natives determined to allow drilling on Native land? Universal Oil, desperate to remove a thorn from their side? Or could the mysterious Carl Bettnor be right, and Dimitri really had been a spy?

And what had she started with Brian? She knew at some cellular level that there was a bond between them, one she didn't want. She wasn't satisfied with his answer to her question as to why he had changed his mind about helping her, but her distrust was somewhat lessened. He couldn't have foretold this. He was in as much danger as she was.

THE FIRE, fed by dried moss and dead limbs, blazed in the hearth, its flames glinting off the dark walls and poking long fingers into the corners of the small enclosure. It's warmth filled the cave. Malinche had taken off her jacket and now stretched out on her sleeping bag close to the penetrating heat.

Brian lay on the opposite side of the fire, his elbow resting on his sleeping bag, staring unseeingly at the flames. Malinche refused to think about their precarious situation; instead, her eyes took in every aspect of the man. Light flickered across his lean features, highlighting his strong nose, leaving dark hollows beneath his cheekbones. Burnished to gold by the fire, his hair fell across his high forehead. She was achingly aware of him, a feeling she didn't try to analyze.

She had been through too much drama in the past few days. She relished this moment when all she had to do was just be. Morning would be time enough to make plans, assess their situation. To think of all the reasons she shouldn't get involved with Brian.

Brian apparently was caught in the same tranquil mood. He smiled lazily, but it caused her pulse to speed up. "Had enough to eat?"

"I never though I'd say this about nuts and raisins, but it was delicious. It was the instant chocolate that put it in the gourmet category, though."

"I took you for a chocolate lover the minute I saw you."

"Did you? I decided you were a rugged type whose favorite beverage was a shot of red-eye."

He chuckled. "I'm more for a Coke, and maybe a quick beer."

"No wine?"

"I don't mind a bottle now and then. What I don't like are the pretensions that usually go with it. Like, what vintage it is, and whether or not you have the correct glass."

They continued the casual conversation, but Malinche's feelings weren't at all casual. Tension lay under the ordinary words, a keen awareness that grew with each second.

Finally she spoke her mind. "Brian, you said you've

never thought of the future. What about the past? Have you ever wanted to marry, have children?''

He hesitated. ''Yes, I've thought of it. But I've never found a woman who could handle my life-style. I like the way I live, but it's too hard for a woman.''

''How do you know? Some women might like that kind of life.''

He raised a skeptical eyebrow. ''Do you know what my life is like? Long weeks in the wild, living out of a backpack. All kinds of weather. The people I meet aren't usually what you'd call trendsetters. It's not a sophisticated life-style. With your background, I doubt you could even conceive of what it's like.''

She started to protest, but hesitated. Perhaps he was right. What did she know about it, except the few things she remembered as a child? After that, her life had been as sheltered as an adoring father with plenty of money could make it.

''That's why I came to Alaska,'' she said, ''to find out what kind of life I belong to. Things haven't always been easy for me—my heritage—''

Brian waved a dismissive hand. ''I don't feel sorry for you because of your heritage. You have the possibility of two worlds. You're not limited, you can take the best from both.''

''If people let you—but they don't. You're an ambiguity and everyone wants to label you. You can't be just an individual—you must fit into a category. Even the census forms don't have a space for biracial. So we're forced to choose, to cut off part of ourselves to let the other part prosper.''

He frowned. ''I guess I never thought much about it.''

''I don't mean to complain. You're right, I'm really

fortunate. It seems a small problem compared to the life-and-death struggles of the people who used to live here.''

Brian rose and walked to the entrance of the cave. ''Do you feel it?'' he said softly. ''I should be planning, thinking, deciding how we're going to get back to the real world, but somehow this cave makes that world seem like a dream.''

''I suppose it's because this place is so ancient,'' she said, rising to stand beside him. ''You can feel those long-ago lives. It brings you back to elemental things. Shelter. Warmth. Food.''

''Love.'' As though it were the most natural thing in the world, he turned and took her in his arms.

In the hidden center of her being, she had been waiting for this, expecting this, wondering how she would respond. For the moment, her suspicions of him were gone, her self-protectiveness forgotten. She moved closer, seeking the warmth and hard tension of his body. Abandoning everything to this moment, she lifted her arms and drew his head down to hers.

His kiss flamed through her every cell; she felt a jolt of desire so powerful that she shuddered under the impact. No forewarning, no gradual building of tenderness and trust, it was just there, like a fierce summer storm, rolling thunder, flashing lightning. She didn't think about it, she didn't question it, she didn't tear it apart with wondering what it meant, what the consequences would be. She allowed it to consume her.

''I want you,'' she whispered into the heated skin of his throat.

He took a deep, tortured breath and tightened his arms around her. ''Are you sure? Do you want me as much as I want you?''

From the husky trembling in his voice, the intensity in his eyes, she knew he, too, had been caught unaware by the ferocity of the storm. She understood, as well, his fear that he would take advantage of her vulnerability. "I'm sure," she murmured.

Then he was kissing her wildly, deeply, claiming her mouth for his, and she mindlessly returned his passion. Her fingers dug deep into his shoulders, pulling him closer. Her hands tore at his clothing, pushing aside his shirt, and she moaned as his hand captured her breast. The soft sound deep in her throat seemed to spur him on. Her legs refused to hold her and she fell against him; he half carried her to the sleeping bag and they tumbled together onto the soft down. A few deft movements, and they were both naked in the heat of the fire.

There were no words, only inarticulate murmurs, choked cries; then there was nothing but the insistent demand of the life force. It grasped them, bent them to its inexorable will. The heat of the fire combined with the heat of their blood, and they came together, wildly, deliriously, joyously.

Long after the initial passion subsided, they lay quietly, her head cradled on his shoulder, his arm thrown across her hip in a tender, possessive gesture.

"I should replenish the fire," he murmured, but he made no move to disengage himself.

She opened her eyes. The firelight glistened on his moist skin, the light and shadow still chased itself across the low ceiling. "Not yet," she whispered. She sensed that this was a moment out of time, and she wanted it to last as long as it could before she would need to dissect it for meaning.

Eventually she stirred. He pulled the sleeping bag up

over her shoulders. "You're so beautiful," he murmured, leaning down to kiss her cheek.

Beautiful. Nothing about what he really thought of her. Nothing about love. But she must mean something to him; he had changed his mind about helping her. "Brian," she said, "why did you change your mind about helping me find Dimitri's killer?"

He hesitated, running the question through his mind. He no longer thought she was involved with the CIA, or that she was hiding anything from him. Perhaps he should level with her. The way he felt now, basking in the aftermath of lovemaking, he wanted to tell her the truth. Or part of it, anyway.

"You weren't the only one having bizarre accidents. My apartment had been searched, I'd had some warnings. I didn't know what to connect them to, until you told me about Dimitri and what was happening to you. Then it seemed somebody was after both of us, and for the same reason. The connection was Dimitri. I figured I didn't have much choice—either I found whoever was jerking us around, or he found me."

He saw the shadow in her eyes and suspected she knew how much he had distrusted her at first. That was no longer true, but it didn't change the larger issue. He couldn't afford to get too deeply involved with Malinche. When this episode was over, and they had run down Dimitri's killer, their idyll would be over. He would accept this wonderful interlude as a gift, the most beautiful he'd ever known, but he knew better than to expect it to last.

BRIAN STOOPED to enter the cave that had become as familiar as his own apartment, and slipped his pack off his shoulder. Malinche was still sleeping, curled like a warm soft rabbit in her sleeping bag. She seemed quite comfortable. It was amazing how during the two days they had been marooned here she had adjusted to the rhythm of the land.

She heard him and raised sleep-heavy eyelids, a slow smile curving her lips. "Brian—I didn't hear you go out."

His heart twisted with something very like pain. She was so utterly desirable. His body reacted, signaling its readiness, as it did each time he saw her. She drew him like a magnet. He went to her immediately and gathered her in his arms, luxuriating in her sleep-warm body.

Everything seemed unreal, and yet in some ways more real than anything he had ever known—the nights of fervent lovemaking, the days of intimate conversation. If they had been anyplace else he knew it would have been different, but both seemed to have silently agreed to savor this moment. It might be all they had. Who knew whether they would survive, and if they did return to the normal world, he suspected they would pick up all their old problems and suspicions. But for now, he knew the meaning of Eden.

When they left the cave— The thought hung over him. They had put off discussing it, and they had to talk about it.

Gently, he unwound his arms from around her and stood up. Thinking was easier the farther away from her he was.

"Malinche, it's time we made some plans...."

She stretched luxuriously, exposing her sweet high breasts, then tilted her head back and lifted her dark hair from her neck, sending it streaming down over her back in a gesture so sensuous, so compelling, that his mouth went dry. He almost wished they *were* back in time, hunters and fighters in a precarious world, and this woman was his to protect and cherish.

He laughed at himself for the thought. This woman was made for civilization, for gentle, easy living, and he'd better not forget it. But their situation was precarious enough; that at least was true.

"Plans?" Malinche echoed. "What can we do? If we step outside, we run the risk of exposing ourselves to the shooter. You said we had no alternative but to wait for rescue. Even if the plane didn't return, you said it was impossible to walk to safety."

"We've heard the plane only once in the past two days. Maybe he's given up, and plans to leave us to the elements. Anyway, we can't stay here much longer. Our food is running out, and I haven't seen any game. Before our supplies are all gone we had better try to walk out. Maybe we can make it—it's a chance."

"Wouldn't we be worse off, blindly striking out onto the tundra? How far are we from a settlement?"

"I don't know exactly. Quite a ways." And the trek would be a gamble no matter how far they had to go. Even he, familiar as he was with the wilderness, would have a hard time. They would have to count on killing game, scarce at this time of year, and the Brooks Range barred the way to Kotzebue. Going back to Barrow was equally unthinkable. They would have to head for the seacoast and hope they ran into a Native village.

Bad for him, nearly impossible for her. But staying here to await slow starvation was impossible.

He cursed himself for allowing her to get into this situation. If they ever *did* get out, he was putting her on the first plane for Seattle if he had to throw her aboard.

She rose to her knees, bent to place a branch on the embers of the fire, and glanced up at him. "We don't have much choice, do we? If we were going to be rescued, it would have happened by now."

He nodded. "Let's stay one more night, then get an early start tomorrow. Although, with the light the way it is, I suppose we could start anytime."

"Let's wait for morning."

He nodded. He desperately wanted one more night with her in this fantasyland before reality intruded.

The day passed as the ones before it, with intimate talk and occasional forays outside the cave, always with their eyes and ears tuned to the sky. Being held captive by an elusive enemy should have infuriated Brian, but he admitted it had its joys. Here they were just a man and a woman, existing at the most elemental level. All everyday problems seemed inconsequential, when life was stripped to its essentials. And Brian was desperately afraid that Malinche was becoming one of the essentials.

Malinche saw the ambivalence in his face, and bent to blow on the fire so he couldn't see her own expression. These few days had shattered her defenses. If she allowed it, she might love this man. Perhaps she already did. She told herself she felt that way because they were imprisoned together in this remote wilderness, removed from all conflict. It would be another story when she faced her old demons.

She hadn't the slightest idea how he felt about her. She knew he loved making love with her. He was both fierce and tender, showing her almost every facet of himself.

Almost. There were times when he drew his reserve around him like armor.

She reached into the backpack and pulled out a cellophane package. "This is the last of the coffee. Do you want some now?"

His hand closed over hers. "Right now I want you."

She came to him eagerly, raising her arm to bring his head down to hers. Their lips met, clung....

She pulled slightly away. "Wait. Do you hear it?"

He raised his head. The faint hum was becoming louder. "It sounds like a plane. Do you suppose he's back? If so, we're still trapped."

"It's possible it's someone else."

Hand in hand, they crept to the entry and peered out. Several hundred yards away their plane still stood, like a bird whose wings had been clipped.

Another plane circled around it, then straightened out to come in for a jerky landing.

"I don't believe it!" Brian gave a jubilant shout. Even from this distance he recognized the squat, heavy figure of George. The man glanced all around, then began waving his arms and shouting.

"It's him!" Brian yelled. "He's come for us. Let's get out of here."

"Wait! What if he's the one who cut the fuel line?"

"Then he wouldn't have come back for us. Come on!"

Grabbing up their packs, Brian made for the door.

Malinche followed more slowly behind him. She never would have believed she could be so torn. They were safe, they were rescued. They would soon be on their way to civilization.

And yet—civilization meant losing this halcyon time, leaving this tiny spot on earth where she had been happier than she had ever been. Or possibly would ever be again.

She paused in the entryway and took one last look at the cave where she had lost her inhibitions, her fears, where she had followed her heart.

She would never see it again, and it hurt more than she would have believed possible.

Chapter Seven

"Hey! What do you guys think you're doing? On vacation or something?" George's face was wreathed in smiles as he ran toward them, his short legs moving fast over the rough terrain.

Brian reached him before Malinche did, and grasped his hand. "Are we ever glad to see you. What took you so long?"

"You didn't leave a map." George glanced from one to the other with a sly smile. "What are you complaining about, anyway? Don't tell me you couldn't find a way to fill the time?"

Malinche hurried to join them. She would never understand the masculine sex. They were laughing and joking as though there had never been the slightest danger. She, at least, would never forget her terror as their plane plummeted to the ground.

Nor would she ever forget the hours of ecstasy. Brian, on the other hand, chatting casually with George, refused to meet her glance, seeming to have forgotten that interlude as well.

She put out her hand to George. "Thank heaven you found us. How did you manage it? There was no answer to our radio call."

"I picked up the call that you had crash-landed—then you cut out. I couldn't tell where you were, and I couldn't get a reply when I called you. So—I just started looking."

Malinche shivered. *I just started looking.* Those simple words said a lot. There was so much territory to cover. Sheer luck must have had a lot to do with their rescue.

As though aware of her thoughts, George shook his head. "I knew pretty well the course you would follow—it just took a while to locate you." He turned back to Brian, all business. "Now, let's take a look at your plane."

The two men moved to the fuel line. Brian gestured, George nodded. Malinche heard the murmur of their voices as she looked back at the cave where she had spent some of her most fearful and happiest hours. In a few minutes it would be nothing but a memory. The knowledge imparted a bittersweet sadness to her relief at being rescued, a poignant feeling of loss.

Brian walked toward her, wiping the grease from his hands on his jeans. "George agrees. There doesn't seem to be anything wrong but a break in the fuel line."

"Did he bring anything to fix it?"

"That's not the problem. The break is easy enough to plug. But he doesn't have enough gas to get both planes to Kotzebue—or back to Barrow. He'll give us a ride to Kotzebue, and I'll come back for the plane. Let's get our stuff aboard."

Malinche tossed her duffel bag into George's plane. The Cessna, the same model as Brian's, looked a little beat-up, but who was she to find fault now? Anything was better than walking.

George grinned at her expression. "She runs like a jewel, miss. Don't worry. She'll get us to Kotzebue."

And she undoubtedly would, Malinche thought. George seemed to be competent in a lot of things Malinche wouldn't have suspected when she met him a few days ago. Apparently sabotage wasn't one of them, though, or he would not have searched for them. Unless the crash wasn't meant to kill them—just scare them enough to make them drop the investigation. Brian didn't think so, but was it conceivable that George had arranged for everything, figuring a couple of days would soften them up?

The theory didn't stand up, though, against the memory of the bullets slamming into the tundra as they ran for the cave. Those bullets were too close; the assailant had been doing his best to kill them.

A few minutes later they were aloft. Malinche looked down at the ground, unexpectedly forlorn. The site was becoming smaller and smaller as the plane gained altitude. Now the cave wasn't even visible in the vast gray-green of the tundra. Was it even there? Was the entire episode a hallucination?

As far as Brian was concerned, it might as well be, she thought sourly. He had hardly touched her, hardly glanced her way, since George had touched his plane down. She could have been a casual acquaintance, not someone who had shared with him an incendiary passion.

Which was fine with her. The episode was best forgotten. It had been an extraordinary time, and neither had reacted as they normally would have. She had forgotten her determination to be free of male domination; and he had acted as though he loved her—although the word *love* had never passed his lips. In spite of their closeness, their passionate intimacy, she had never penetrated his deep reserve. She had been very close to loving him. Perhaps she actually had, for a brief moment. But the moment out of time had passed, the fantasy was over.

She mustn't lose sight of her primary purpose—to find out who had killed her brother and to make that person pay. Brian was important only to the extent he could help her do that.

She glanced at his profile, a sight now imprinted on her heart. His jaw was set, his eyes focused straight ahead. His macho-man armor was back in place. It was obvious from his manner that making love again wasn't anything she had to worry about.

Brian felt her glance, a warm touch that sent his pulse racing, and he held tight to his reserve. He had known when he first saw her that she could be dangerous to his peace of mind. She might be capable of upsetting all his assumptions. But nothing could overcome the fact that she belonged to a gentler, softer place than he could ever provide. Would ever want to provide. If he wasn't careful, she'd be leading him around by a necktie.

During the interlude of sheer happiness in the cave, he had kept such thoughts from his mind. He had known, although he hoped to keep the knowledge from Malinche, that they might never get out alive, and he had grasped for happiness. But now they were returning to the real world, the world where men killed, women betrayed, and the only safety was to trust only oneself.

Yet if he stayed too close to her, he might forget that. The solution was to erect a barrier. He would drop her in Kotzebue and salvage his plane. Then he would make sure she returned to Seattle. He could find the killer faster if he didn't have to worry about her. He'd drop the whole thing himself, if he could, but he knew someone out there wouldn't let him.

George's voice on the radio to Kotzebue control personnel broke into his reverie.

The plane bumped to a landing, and Brian gave a muffled curse. Two men were rushing across the tarmac toward them.

"What the hell is Joe Pasco doing here?"

Malinche's gaze followed his to the short dark man huffing toward him, the same man who had so opportunely been at the pier when they left Anchorage. "Your boss?"

"Looks like. I never saw half as much of him when I was working in Anchorage," Brian muttered. "George, do you have any idea what he's doing here?"

"When you radioed for help, I called your office— I figured they'd be concerned. Did I do the wrong thing?"

"Of course not." Brian swung open the door and jumped down on the tarmac, then lifted his hand up to Malinche. She evaded it skillfully and stepped down beside him.

"Brian, thank God you're safe. You had us worried." Joe Pasco, smiling and expansive, held out his hand.

"I must have, to get you out of the comforts of town," Brian said easily. "You've met Malinche Adams." He glanced significantly at the man standing to the left and slightly behind Pasco.

"Yes, of course. Glad to see you safe, Miss. This is Jim Wilson," Pasco said. "Out of our Denver office." He gave no further explanation, and Brian scanned

Wilson with curiosity. He had never heard the name before, but that meant nothing. He could easily have forgotten. Jim Wilson seemed almost a generic name, and the man himself seemed to fit it: average height, regular features, an unassuming, almost self-deprecating attitude, which made Pasco's deferential manner when he introduced the man rather curious.

Pasco turned to George, his manner much more authoritative. "I have a car here—I'll take these two to rooms I've reserved downtown. Can we drop you anyplace?"

George hesitated, then shook his head. Pasco and his friend had taken control of them very smoothly, Brian thought. He spoke quickly. "I'd like to go back to my plane tomorrow, George. Could you be here in the morning to take me back?"

"Sure." George threw the bags down from the plane, and the three—Pasco, Brian and Malinche—hoisted them to their shoulders. Wilson strode ahead to lead the way to the automobile parked near the terminal.

Malinche didn't join in the conversation on the way to the hotel in downtown Kotzebue. Her mind didn't register the narrow streets lined with low buildings, or the few pedestrians who gazed after their vehicle. In only a few minutes they pulled up in front of the hotel, a two-story, frame structure. She hadn't realized how exhausted she was until she entered the warmth of the rustic lobby.

As they approached the desk, she glanced quickly around. It was more welcoming than she had at first thought, with logs blazing in a huge fireplace, and comfortable chairs pulled up in front of it. All she wanted now, though, was rest. It was quickly arranged to take her bag to her room; she plodded slowly up the narrow stairway, with a glance back over her shoulder at Brian, who followed closely.

He entered her room behind her and scrutinized the surroundings. He wasn't going to take any chances on an ambush. Everything seemed ordinary and safe: the sparsely furnished room; the bed with the green comforter standing in the middle of a beige carpet; the dresser along one planked wall; the bedside table with a reading lamp.

He strode to the door and made a quick survey of the bath—a shower stall and utilitarian sink. Only then, assured that she was alone in her room, did he move toward the door.

"You look exhausted," he said, taking in the dark shadows under her eyes, the slump of her delicate shoulders. A wave of tenderness washed over him; she looked so sweet, so vulnerable. His heart twisted in his chest. He'd have to be careful. Her vulnerability called to his protectiveness, and he didn't want that. Nevertheless, it was all he could do to stay on his own side of the room.

"Thanks," she said dryly. "That always makes a woman feel better." She sank down on the soft bed, a wan smile on her face. "But you're right, I'm tired. I think I could sleep for a week. What are you going to do?"

"I'm going to have a good sleep, too. And a huge meal, maybe not in that order. Tomorrow George will take me out to rescue my plane."

He hesitated. Could he really order her out of his life? His impulse was to take her in his arms and never let her go. Perhaps that was why his voice was harsher than he had intended.

"And I don't want you here when I get back. There's a plane out for Anchorage tomorrow—you can change there for Seattle."

Her eyes shot fire. "I told you. That's not up for discussion."

"I won't have you in danger. Look what's nearly happened to you already."

"*You* won't have me in danger! You have nothing to say about it."

"Don't be stubborn. I can handle this by myself."

She took a deep breath. "Brian, I've told you before. I make my own decisions."

"Fine!" He left the room, slamming the door behind him. He walked slowly to his room, relief that she wouldn't leave vying with fear for her.

He steeled himself to enter his room, knowing Pasco and Wilson would be waiting. Had they really flown up here to assure themselves of his safety, or was there another motive? And how could he think such a thing? He had known Pasco for years; if not an intimate friend, he was at least a business friend.

When he opened the door, Pasco was sitting on the bed. Wilson was at the window, gazing out at the narrow main street of the town. Both turned at his entrance.

Pasco glanced at Wilson, almost as though seeking permission, then gave Brian a hearty smile, "I can't tell you how happy we are to see you safe, pal."

"Yeah, I'm pretty happy about it myself." Brian shut the door and stood with his back to it, his arms folded across his chest. He would let them lead the way. Neither one had asked him about the circumstances that had caused him to set his plane down in the middle of the wilderness. Why not, unless they already knew?

He had better stop such paranoid thinking. It wasn't unreasonable that they were here. George had radioed the information to the tower that he had found them, and had given a short explanation of what had happened.

"Well, at least it's over, no real harm done," Wilson said.

"Just a good scare for all of us," Pasco agreed. "Once you get back to Anchorage, everything will be back to normal. When are you going back?"

A sharpness in Pasco's tone belied the casual question. Brian shrugged. "I'm not sure. I have to salvage my plane tomorrow...."

Pasco nodded. "Then you'll fly back to Anchorage the day after."

"I'm not sure just yet what we'll do." Brian's stubborn streak was surfacing under Pasco's prodding. Pasco was pushing and he didn't know why. And how naturally he, Brian, had said "we" instead of "I." "Malinche wants to stay on a few days—".

Wilson moved from the window, giving Pasco a sharp glance. Who the hell was this man? Pasco was reacting like a puppet on strings. Wilson had been introduced as a Universal Oil man, but Brian was almost sure he hadn't seen him before. Or had he? The man's features were eminently forgettable, his manner so unobtrusive you could almost forget he was there—almost. Brian sensed something deep and hidden under the bland facade.

"Do you think that's a good idea?" Pasco persisted. "If she wants to go on a wild-goose chase, there's no reason for you to go along with it."

At Brian's sharp glance, he spread his hands, palms upward, and shrugged. "I know, I know—it's your business. But did you ever think you might be getting into something you don't know anything about?"

Brian's lips tightened. "If you know so much about it, why don't you tell me what I'm getting into, Joe?"

"Hey—all I know is nothing good can come of prying around into that Native's accidental death."

"Accidental? You know better than that, don't you, Joe?"

"Well, sure, I've heard the rumors. But, so what? If somebody killed him, it was probably one of his own people. He was dead set against the Natives agreeing to let us drill on their lands. And some of his people didn't like that at all."

"No more than Universal Oil did, I suspect."

"What are you implying? That we'd murder to get drilling rights? You've worked for us a long time, and I never thought I'd hear anything like that from you. Are you accusing me—"

"It's not an unreasonable idea," Wilson interposed quietly. "Kennedy was just taking a shot in the dark. No reason to get upset. But I assure you, Kennedy, that whatever happened to Dimitri was none of our doing."

Brian took a deep breath and unclenched his fists. He wouldn't accept Wilson's assurance alone, but he couldn't believe his company for whom he felt a strong loyalty would do something so blatantly criminal. "Sorry."

"So, you'll rescue your plane, rest up a bit, and get on back where you belong?" Pasco asked. "The girl wouldn't be fool enough to stay here by herself."

Brian merely looked at him.

"I've never known you to be so stubborn, man. I'd hate to phrase that as an order."

"I'm on vacation," Brian reminded him.

"Yeah, and I can revoke that anytime. Brian, what's got into you? You've always been a man to mind your own business. You'd never have got involved if it hadn't been for that woman."

Joe rose from the bed and took a step or two toward Brian, shaking his head. "Come on, I know she's a good-looking woman, and with all that time alone, she must have been persuasive—"

"That's enough." Brian's swift surge of fury surprised them all—even himself. But Pasco had no right to imply that about Malinche.

"Damn it, be reasonable! There's a lot involved here, stuff none of us know all about. And you— you've always been levelheaded, practical. You're the last man I'd expect to lose his head over a woman— and a Native fox at that."

Brian stepped forward smoothly, his rage showing only in his eyes. His fist connected with Pasco's jaw, sending the man sprawling on the floor. "You can't talk about her like that."

Joe looked up, an aggrieved expression on his face, as Brian leaned over him, ready to knock him back down.

Jim Wilson, a half smile on his narrow features, stepped between the two men. "That's enough, Kennedy. I'm sure he's sorry." He glanced down at Joe, who was rubbing his chin.

"Yeah," Pasco mumbled, "yeah, I'm sorry." He stumbled toward the bed.

Wilson placed his hand on Brian's arm. "We've been out of line here, Kennedy. We both apologize.

Naturally, Universal Oil doesn't control your private life. We'll be going and let you get some rest.''

His temper still barely under control, Brian nodded curtly. ''Apology accepted. Will you two be returning on the next flight to Anchorage?''

''Oh, I doubt it,'' Wilson said. ''I've never been to Kotzebue before. We might hang around a few days, look the place over. There's bound to be some interesting things to see around here.''

Brian watched the two leave the room, then shut the door carefully behind them. One thing was sure—Universal Oil was interested in Dimitri's death, whether or not they had actually caused it. And had Pasco and Wilson come all this way just to assure themselves of his safety? Or had they been following him since he left Anchorage?

Brian wasn't accustomed to the suspicions that raced through his mind, and he didn't like it. He thought of himself as an honest man with integrity. Up until a few days ago he would have bet anything that the company he worked for was the same.

He was still shaken by the depth of his fury at Joe. He had wanted to kill the man. A basic need to protect Malinche had seemed to come out of nowhere. And that was scary!

Pasco and Wilson didn't need to convince him of the dangers of digging into this thing. He knew it, but he also knew it was too late to drop it.

The greater danger was Malinche—being near her when all his survival instincts told him to get away. The days in the cave had been so idyllic that he might even persuade himself that there was a chance for them—that although she was rich, unused to hardship, would leave when the chips were down, she *might* be

different. That way lay heartbreak. He could face a
grizzly, could face a gun, but he knew any relationship
with Malinche would be temporary. He would come to
love her and she would be gone. That he couldn't face.
Better not let it happen in the first place.

If it wasn't already too late. He had to admit he'd
felt a surge of relief when she had refused to leave;
staying near her would be tough, but it was better than
her absence. No, he'd see this through. He would just
be sure that nothing more occurred between them.

He forced his thoughts back to Wilson and Pasco.
They had sure changed their minds about staying in
Kotzebue. Interesting things to see, indeed!

MALINCHE HAULED HERSELF off the bed and into the
small bathroom. Standing under the shower, she closed
her eyes and allowed the warmth to penetrate her aching muscles and flow like balm over her skin. The jade
dragon hung between her breasts and she fingered it
lightly, taking comfort in its familiarity.

She toweled slowly and luxuriously, then slipped on
a light silk gown whose collar reached just under her
chin, but which clung like a second skin. It had seemed
an unnecessary item on such a rugged trip, but it took
up so little room she had given in to the impulse.

Had Brian been in her mind when she packed it?
Probably, she admitted. She pulled the heavy shades to
darken the room, and then slid between the cotton
sheets and pulled the comforter up around her neck.

The sleep she courted was not to be. Tired as her
body was, her mind pulsed with energy. Over and over
she relived the past few days, but every time she tried
to concentrate on who was menacing her, her thoughts

returned to those days and nights with Brian in the ancient cave.

Another time, another place, she might have loved him with all her soul. But she was a wanderer between two worlds, pulled by two different cultures, and until she resolved that dichotomy, she could not truly love anyone. She was glad he had tried to order her about; it deepened her realization of the chasm between them. She might not know where she belonged, but she did know something about herself. The man she loved would treat her as an equal, not a recalcitrant child.

Finally she drifted off, only to jolt wide-awake again. She wasn't sure what had awakened her. It wasn't a sound. It was more that she sensed a presence in her room, a scent of danger. Instantly she was wide-awake, every muscle rigid as she listened.

Her heart was pounding so loud she suspected it could be heard a mile away. Making a supreme effort, she slowed her breathing, making sure that it continued its calm, even rhythm that would indicate she slept. Slowly, ever so slowly, she opened her eyelids a fraction of an inch. She could see nothing. The drawn shades kept out the light of the midnight sun.

Suddenly a gloved hand closed over her mouth, choking off her scream. Another hand captured her hands, holding them in a tight, cruel grip.

"Don't make a sound." The voice was muffled, unrecognizable.

She struggled briefly, but the pressure on her arms tightened, sending pain shooting along her arms.

"Where is it?" the voice hissed.

She tried to respond, but the hand effectively cut off all sound. Anger shot through her, mixing with the fear.

How did the fool expect an answer if he wouldn't let her speak?

The question had apparently been rhetorical, anyway. She squirmed as he fastened duct tape over her mouth and secured her arms behind her back.

Wide-eyed with terror, she watched the dark form go to her bag and dump the contents on the floor. He sorted through the contents, throwing things in all directions. Even in the partial darkness she might have been able to recognize him, but he wore black clothing and a ski mask obliterated his features.

He made a quick, systematic search of the rest of the room, dumping out drawers, checking the pockets of her jeans. She tried to memorize every detail of his appearance, but all she could tell for sure was that he was a man of medium size, medium build. She could never recognize him if she saw him again.

With a curse, he threw her backpack onto the floor at the foot of her bed. Whatever he was searching for, he had obviously not found it. Could it be the dragon? The long chain kept the tiny object out of sight beneath her gown.

"I'm going to warn you one more time," he whispered. "Drop this Dimitri thing. Or you could wind up right where he is."

He yanked the tape from her wrists. "Just forget you ever saw me here," he muttered. "It should take you a few seconds to get the tape off your mouth. If I hear one shout, one scream, I'll be back in here and I won't be so gentle. Understand?" He gave a hard yank on her arm. "I should kill you now, but your boyfriend and his pals are too close."

She nodded frantically; she wasn't sure she *could* move. She watched his dark form move to the door and an eternity later heard the door close behind him. Only then did she take a deep breath.

She yanked the tape from her lips. Her first impulse was to scream, but what if he actually was waiting on the other side of the door? He could reach her long before anyone else could, and she believed his promise to harm her if she alerted anyone.

She could run down the hall and find Brian, but she wasn't sure which room was his. It would be too dangerous to stumble into just any room. Besides, what could he do? The intruder would be long gone before she could alert Brian. Or, she thought, shuddering, he could have removed his disguise and be right among them.

How had the man got in here, anyway? She was sure she had locked the door—she always did.

She slid from the bed and crept across to the door. Nothing had been broken; apparently the man had a passkey or else was adept at picking locks. She locked the door again, wishing she had more trust in its ability to keep out intruders.

What had the man been after? Whatever it was, he hadn't found it. Her hand touched the talisman between her breasts. Did he want the dragon? If so, why? It was like any of a dozen for sale at any craft shop. She resolved that in the morning, she would examine the dragon even more carefully, although she didn't expect to see anything she hadn't seen before.

There was nothing to be done until morning. She wouldn't test his warning about keeping her mouth shut. She could call the authorities, she supposed, but so far they hadn't been interested in anything she told them.

Briefly she thought of going immediately to Brian,

but she hesitated. He'd been so angry when he left so determined to make her leave. This would only confirm his belief that she was in danger, and even if he couldn't force her to leave, he might stop helping her.

And there was nothing he could do now. The man was long gone.

She'd talk it over with Brian tomorrow. He had planned to leave early to salvage his plane. It was 4:00 a.m. now. She would be up by five and catch him before he left.

The plan allowed her to relax, and exhaustion caused her to doze. When she woke again, she glanced at the clock and jerked wide awake. Nine o'clock. Brian was gone.

Chapter Eight

Malinche slipped into a booth in the hotel's coffee shop and looked around at the other customers. Few people were here this late in the morning: several men clustered around a table in the center of the room drinking coffee and talking loudly; an elderly couple, apparently tourists, in one of the booths; four teenagers in another booth, who, considering their features and Native dress, were Eskimo. No one looked in the least threatening.

She'd known Brian would be gone when she checked her watch on awakening, but she had checked at the front desk to be sure. The clerk confirmed he'd left around six.

She gave her order to a smiling teenage waitress with straight dark hair and flashing eyes who made a production of passing by the youths in the other booth. In spite of her own concerns, Malinche smiled. The girl was obviously the reason for the young men's presence.

Even though she'd known Brian wouldn't be here, she had to stifle a sharp pang of disappointment. She was alone in a strange place, suspicious of everyone, at the mercy of an enemy she didn't know. She had never felt so terribly vulnerable.

But there was nothing to be done about it. She had an entire day to fill before Brian returned, and she could hardly go back to her room, lock the door, and pull the covers over her head. And she couldn't sit here, frozen with fear, a woman unable to move without a man. She should get on with the job she had come to do.

Two men entering the room caught her attention. She remembered the names—Joe Pasco and Jim Wilson—the men who had met their plane, co-workers of Brian's. They glanced around the room, started toward a booth, then caught sight of her.

"Miss Adams, I hope you had a good night's rest." Joe Pasco came to her booth, smiling expansively.

Malinche trusted no one; she listened carefully to the tone of his voice. Had she heard it last night, muffled by a ski mask? Impossible to tell. Nevertheless, the man had a habit of turning up when least expected. It was best to be cautious.

"Yes, thank you. I'm afraid I overslept. I haven't been outside yet."

"I doubt you missed much," Wilson said. "We've been out looking over the town, and it didn't take long."

"Won't you join me?" The offer was perfunctory, and she was relieved when the men thanked her, but moved on to another table.

Trying not to be too obvious, she watched them out of the corner of her eye. They bent their heads close together, apparently discussing a private matter. Nothing unusual; lots of people didn't care to announce their business in a public place. She wondered, though, if she was the subject of their discussion.

Seeing them now, two seemingly ordinary businessmen consuming a breakfast of eggs and hash brown potatoes, it didn't seem realistic to believe either was a thug who would break into her bedroom. Yet who else knew of her presence here? And more, that she was in possession of something someone wanted badly.

She wished she knew what it was. The dragon that hung heavy and warm between her breasts? She had scrutinized it carefully, and although something about it seemed different, she couldn't put her finger on it. Or could it be the envelope from the Department of the Army that they had discovered among Dimitri's files? Neither seemed incriminating. What was she missing?

She patted her wallet, secure in the knowledge that the envelope was still hidden in the secret compartment, missed by the intruder. As clues went, it wasn't much, but it was all she had.

She took her check to the counter and gazed thoughtfully at the cashier who was also the waitress. She appeared to be a Native; would she have known Dimitri?

The two men still sitting in the booth behind her made up her mind. She didn't want them listening to her questions. She could talk to the girl later.

She stepped out into the street, bracing herself against the chill. Patches of snow still clung to the sides of the walkway. A bitter wind blew down the narrow black-topped street, and she drew her jacket more closely around her. Spring in Kotzebue could have passed for winter in nearly any other place.

A few people, some clad in mukluks and fur parkas, others in modern nylon down jackets, strode briskly along the walkway. Shops—a clothing store, a bar— were open, but didn't seem to be doing much business.

Since she didn't know where to begin, this was as good as any.

She went into the first shop—Kotzebue Mercantile—and wandered to a rack of fur parkas. Riffling through them, she surveyed the store. She was the only one here. A few minutes later a tall thin man, probably in his fifties, with blue eyes and a white beard, moved toward her.

"Something I can help you with?"

"Oh, I'm just looking—" She paused. "Actually, I'm looking for someone who might have known a friend of mine."

"I've lived here for twenty years. Who is your friend?"

"He was a Native artist. Dimitri Stanislof. I heard he was here attending the Eskimo rendezvous." She watched closely for a flicker in his eyes, an uneasy movement, but there was nothing.

"Dimitri Stanislof. Seems I heard the name someplace, but I'm not sure. I never met him, anyway. If he was at the rendezvous, he might not have been here in town. That's a few miles farther out on the coast. But you might ask over at the Northern Lights Bar. Fellow who runs it is an Eskimo."

"Thanks." Malinche walked the few yards to the Northern Lights Bar. She was probably going to get nowhere, but at least it would fill the time until Brian returned. And she might get lucky.

She glanced over her shoulder, half expecting to see Pasco and Wilson ambling along behind her, but the walk was empty. She would have almost preferred to see them. It would account for her feeling of menace, her sense that her every move was watched.

The Eskimo tending bar was also the owner. He listened to her query, then shook his head. "Sorry. I never heard of him."

It was the same in the next few places. Sometimes she thought she detected a hesitation before the reply, but the reply was always the same. No one had known Dimitri.

That seemed strange. The town wasn't that large and most of the people seemed to know each other, judging from the greetings on the street. Perhaps Dimitri hadn't come into town, and had spent all his time at the rendezvous.

She reviewed what she'd heard of the rendezvous. The Gathering had gone on for centuries, Eskimos from Siberia and Greenland meeting with friends and relatives in Alaska once a year for trading, visiting, renewing old ties. During the Cold War both the United States and Russia had forbidden travel to the other side. When tensions eased, the event was joyously renewed.

Why had Dimitri come here? Had he really been a spy? With the Cold War over, why would anyone be spying, anyway? He'd told George he'd come here looking for someone...someone dangerous.

It was late afternoon when she entered the Whale's Tail Bar and Lunchroom. The aroma of frying meat reminded her that it had been a long time since breakfast. She glanced at the bar. It was empty except for the heavy woman bartender. She found a table at the far end from which she could see the specials listed on a blackboard.

When the bartender came for her order, she asked her usual question and received the usual negative answer, then ordered her sandwich. Waiting, she glanced around the darkened interior. Except for a Native at a far table, she was alone.

So, why didn't she feel alone?

She sighed, sipping the coffee the woman had thoughtfully brought her. She had wasted an entire day with fruitless questions. Maybe Dimitri hadn't even come to Kotzebue; perhaps he had told George that to cover his trail. Or perhaps George—

"Mind if I sit down?"

Startled, she jiggled her coffee cup, spilling some of the liquid on the oilcloth-covered table. The man she had seen sitting at the far table was standing beside her.

She took in his appearance at a glance—a Native, wearing the traditional garb—leather boots, a fur parka open in the warmth of the room. He had coarse black hair and black eyes. Her pulse slowed; he didn't appear threatening.

He didn't wait for a reply, but glanced over his shoulder, then slid into a chair. "What are you asking questions about Dimitri for?"

Her heart leaped with excitement; her quest was finally paying off. She answered his question with one of her own. "Did you know him?"

"I said, why are you asking?" His eyes narrowed to slits and his gaze bored into hers. He would give nothing until he was sure.

She studied him closely. His eyes held a clear intelligence as well as wariness and he was frowning—a worried frown.

"He was my brother," she said simply, her voice cracking.

The man hesitated. "I'm Charlie Frank. He was my friend."

She stared at him and he stared back. A standoff. He was taking her measure, wondering how far to trust her.

"If you are his sister you must know he's dead," he said. "You're not looking for him. What are you really doing here?"

"I know he's dead. I want to find out why—and who killed him."

"So, you don't think it was an accident, like they say."

"No. I don't think anybody really believes that. There's a cover-up, but I don't know why." She pulled the envelope from her wallet. "Dimitri was apparently corresponding with the Department of Defense. Do you know why?"

Charlie stared at the envelope, then glanced furtively around the room. "We need to talk. But not now. Not here."

"Where, then?" She leaned eagerly toward him.

"I'll meet you tonight at the rendezvous camp."

"How can I find you in a crowd?"

"There's not much of a crowd there now. Most everybody comes by dogsled across the ice and goes home before the ice breaks up. I'll find you."

She opened her mouth to ask another question, but he was gone as quickly as a shadow.

"Here's your sandwich, Miss."

"Thank you." Malinche's eyes were still on the door through which Charlie had just vanished. "Do you know that man?"

"Charlie Frank? Sure. He lives out at the Eskimo village. He wasn't bothering you, was he?"

"Oh, no, not at all." Malinche munched on her sandwich, making her plans. She could easily find out where the village was, but she didn't want to go alone. Charlie's eyes had registered fear when he glanced around the room. He had been hesitant to talk to her.

As much as she wanted to be independent, to show Brian he couldn't boss her around, it was wiser to wait for him.

She was sitting in the lobby of the hotel when Brian swung through the doors, lean and vital and exciting. It was ridiculous how her heart leaped in her chest and her throat tightened just at the sight of him. His gaze swept the lobby, ignoring the stuffed caribou heads with the sightless eyes, the baleen fastened to the wall, and came to rest on her. He halted in midstride, as though unable to take his eyes from her. An elemental force seemed to arc between them, holding them both very still. Then he broke the spell and strode across the bear hides covering the floor to her side.

"I see you're still here. I thought you might have changed your mind." In spite of his brusque words, she thought she saw relief in his eyes. Was he glad she had stayed?

"No way. But I did find out a few things. Are you starving, or can we go someplace and talk?"

A hint of wariness showed in his eyes. What egotism. Did he think she wanted to talk about their relationship? If he didn't wish to discuss it, she certainly didn't, either.

Yet they had to acknowledge what had happened. They couldn't continue to shy away, neither mentioning what was paramount on both their minds. On hers, anyway, she admitted.

"Let's go into the lounge," he said. "I'd like a beer."

The bar, almost deserted at this time of day, was a good choice for an intimate conversation. Brian chose a table near the back, and pulled out her chair. "Will this do?"

She surveyed the room, satisfied that no one could overhear. She had seen no one following her, but she had never gotten over the feeling that she was under surveillance.

She had meant to tell Brian immediately about the intruder in her bedroom. She had been bursting to tell him ever since it happened. In light of this, she was surprised by the words that actually came out of her mouth.

"Brian—about what happened in the cave—"

He glanced down at his hands, refusing to meet her eyes. "I'm sorry about that, Malinche. I apologize. I should never have taken advantage of you when you were so frightened and vulnerable."

Apologize! The nerve of him! The words were insulting, an affront to her intelligence and will. She wasn't a child, taken advantage of and seduced by an older, wiser man. She wasn't prey. She made her own decisions.

"I wasn't *that* frightened," she said coldly. "If you'll recall, I made the first move."

"Then let's say it was mutual. It happened because of the time and place and circumstance. Perhaps it's something we should put behind us. Neither of us planned it."

Put it behind him, as easily as that? She'd meant nothing to him? Damn him, she certainly wasn't going to admit it had meant more to her. "I'm glad you feel that way. We weren't ourselves. It can't lead to anything. I just wanted to be sure you knew that."

It hurt to think the man with whom she'd experienced the most wonderful moments of her life could just forget it, but it was better this way. They both saw it for what it was, a lovely interlude, not something to build a life on.

"Was that what you wanted to talk about?"

"Yes. No." She stumbled over the words. "I wanted to tell you about my nighttime visitor." As she told Brian all that had happened, his gray eyes darkened to near black. When she finished, he reached across the table and grasped her hand. "Did he hurt you? Are you all right?"

"Yes, I'm fine. I was frightened, but I'm over that now. He was after something, and he wanted it badly." She leaned forward, her eyes bright with excitement. "And we may be close to finding out what it is. I did some investigating today."

His grip tightened until she winced. "Out alone asking questions?" he exploded. "After being assaulted in your own room. How dumb can you be! Malinche, this isn't a game. Anything could have happened to you. You could have been killed. You should have waited for me."

"Brian, I didn't ask you to help me so you could take care of me or make my decisions for me. Dimitri was *my* brother, and I'm responsible for finding out who killed him."

"Yeah, well, just remember somebody wants to kill me, too."

"Okay, I can't do it without you, I know, but please remember, I asked you to *help,* not take over."

"I'd have made sure you stayed in Anchorage if I'd known you would take such fool chances."

They stared at each other across the table. Brian appeared to be as angry as she was. As she stared into his eyes, her anger slipped away, replaced by a cold knowledge. Brian couldn't help feeling that he always had to be in charge. It was part of him.

She withdrew her hand from his and sighed. "I'm sorry I worried you. But let me tell you what I found out."

Brian frowned as she related her conversation with Charlie Frank. "Can you trust him?"

"I don't know. He seemed sincere. I don't think he liked my asking questions about Dimitri at first. I'm not sure he was going to tell me anything until he saw the envelope. That must mean something. And he was very nervous. He kept looking around as though he expected to see a demon come out of the woodwork."

Brian took a deep, ragged breath. The woman drove him absolutely crazy with her inability to understand the kind of danger she was in. Running around town alone asking questions about a murdered man, when she had already been run down by a car, shot at, and attacked in her room, was asking for trouble. And if anything happened to her—

He cut off the thought. It didn't bear thinking about. But she had certainly seemed eager to dismiss their lovemaking. How coldly she'd told him to forget it. Now that she'd had time to think about it, she realized she'd made a mistake, what life with him would be like. He was lucky she'd realized it before any harm had been done. Before he had learned to love her, for example.

So why did it hurt so much?

THE FOUR-WHEELER sped across the tundra, bumping and slipping on spots of still-frozen ground. Malinche, placing her cheek against the back of Brian's down parka, was glad he was in front to deflect the wind.

The solid feel of his body gave her a sense of security, even knowing it was an illusion. She chanced a glance around. Although wildflowers were blooming in places that only a few days ago were still covered with ice and the sun shone down from a cloudless sky, summer in the arctic was relative.

Conversation wasn't possible over the roar of the motor. To her, the flat, bleak landscape looked featureless and foreboding. The sea was out there somewhere, blending into the land, but she couldn't say exactly where one ended and the other began.

The desolate landscape didn't seem to bother Brian. He'd made a few inquiries, hired a vehicle, and they were now on their way to the Eskimo rendezvous camp located at the edge of the sea.

They heard the village almost as soon as they saw it. A cacophony of barking dogs announced their arrival. As Brian skidded to a stop, she gazed with keen interest around the settlement. The wooden houses grouped on the shore of the Bering Strait marked the village as permanent, although several tents a short distance away attested to a partial nomadic life-style.

The sun made the bleak landscape almost pleasant, as it glistened off the rocky shore and fingered the ice floes in the process of cracking apart. Several hundred yards out the sea was visible, streaks of intense blue appearing between huge fields of solid ice, while closer to shore, chunks of ice surged and ground against each other in constant complaint.

She was surprised that no one came to greet them. The dogs had certainly announced them, and in her experience, everyone always rushed out to greet visitors.

"Where did Charlie say he'd meet you?" Brian

asked, his expression puzzled as he glanced at the empty houses.

"He didn't say precisely—just that he'd meet me at this village. He said he'd find me. I assumed he'd meet me or send someone to bring me to him."

Brian started the engine and they cruised slowly down the narrow strip between the short row of houses. "I'm beginning to get a bad feeling about this," he said, more to himself than to Malinche.

She didn't reply. She, too, was beginning to feel that something sinister was going on. Had Charlie led them into a trap? How could an empty village be a trap? Or had he planned to get them here in order to divert them from something else? None of that seemed reasonable. She remembered the fear in his eyes, the furtive way he had glanced over his shoulder when he whispered the meeting place. Charlie was afraid of something.

"Wait," she shouted into Brian's ear. "I think I see something over there."

Brian brought the four-wheeler to a halt, and he gazed in the direction she pointed to.

"Yeah. It looks like our missing villagers."

A large group of people huddled along the shoreline, milling about and gesturing at something at their feet, something invisible at this distance to Malinche.

"Maybe somebody killed a whale or a walrus," Brian said, speeding toward the group.

As they neared the knot of people, it became clear to Malinche that whatever had brought the Eskimos to the shore wasn't a happy occasion. Instead of eager shouts of triumph, she caught the sound of high-pitched wailing.

Several people glanced up at their arrival, but made no move to speak. Brian and Malinche pushed their way through the crowd, then stopped abruptly at the sight of the figure sprawled on the sand at their feet.

A terrible knowledge rose in Malinche when she saw the figure crumpled like a piece of driftwood on the shore. The man was obviously dead.

The men were already lifting the body, exposing the battered face Malinche had known she would see. She gave a strangled cry.

"It's—it's Charlie!"

"You knew him?" A large woman with tears in her eyes turned to Malinche. "You were a friend?"

Malinche. "I was a friend. I hadn't known him long, but yes, I was a friend. What happened?"

"An accident, they say." The woman's lips curled in disbelief. "He was out in his kayak, hunting seal, I suppose. Although he didn't tell anyone he was going. He got caught between two ice floes and was crushed to death."

"Did anyone see it happen?"

"No. And he was the best hunter in the village. Not foolhardy, either."

"Did he usually go out alone?"

The woman hesitated. "Sometimes. I'd have thought he would let someone know, though."

She moved to put her arms around another woman who was crying noisily, and the two moved toward the retreating villagers. Malinche glanced up at Brian. "What do you think?"

"I think it's strange that he'd be out looking for seal at this time of year—and just when he agreed to meet you," he said slowly. "And it's odd that an experienced hunter would get caught between two ice floes—although I suppose it could happen."

"Especially," Malinche said softly, "if he happened to be dead before he got crushed."

In the circle of Brian's arm, Malinche scanned the faces around them. Grieving faces, angry faces, good simple faces of good simple people. Was there someone hiding in that crowd who was evil? A murderer?

She shivered and pressed closer to Brian; he seemed an anchor in a tossing sea. It was chilling to think that if there was a murderer in that crowd, he knew them, and might have them next on his list.

Chapter Nine

Malinche and Brian stood apart from the villagers. They were outsiders, two people who had come upon a tragic moment in the lives of these people. To Malinche and Brian, Charlie had been a means to an end. To his friends, his relatives, he had been an integral part of their lives.

One of the men rushed to an old and weathered shed sitting alone on the shore, decrepit but still standing. He pushed in a door, allowing a glimpse of kayaks and oil barrels thrown haphazardly about, and emerged pulling a worn sled. Brian guessed the shelter was used for old and abandoned equipment.

Pulling the sled, the man approached the body which still sprawled on the tundra. A woman took off her fur parka and spread it on the sled. Four men lifted the body gently and reverently and placed it on the sled on top of the fur. Someone else covered it, and everyone gazed silently at the still form.

An elderly man spoke in a language Brian didn't understand. His comments provoked a protest from a woman and two men, and the conversation became general. The group, men and women, formed a small, constantly changing knot around the sled, oblivious to the outsiders. Several were gesticulating forcefully, others raising their voices in heated argument. A discussion was going on, and apparently everyone was not in agreement.

"What are they talking about?" Malinche whispered.

"You got me. There seems to be a disagreement about Charlie." Brian shifted his stance, instinctively aligning his body to shelter Malinche from the wind. The damned, never-ending wind. There were times when even he, as much as he loved the northland, tired of the fierceness of the arctic weather.

But the wind had its compensations. Malinche stood with her back to Brian's chest, pressing closely into his embrace. He tightened his arms around her waist, and lowered his head to take in the crisp, clean smell of her hair. Then he raised the hood of her jacket and tucked it warmly around her face, feeling a fierce protectiveness. How had she become so necessary to him in such a short time?

A cold foreboding gripped him, as he felt the imprint of her body against his chest, his belly, his thighs. Her soft buttocks pressed against the hardness of his body, setting off spasms of response. She was a lightning rod for trouble; could he keep her safe until he got her back to her home?

Even through layers of clothing he sensed her vitality, her pure animal aliveness. Desire shot through him like a beam of incandescent light, and he tightened his grip convulsively, even as his unease grew. He had to keep his head, not give in to the delicious undercurrent of desire. This wasn't the time to even think about it. He could shelter Malinche from the wind, but how could he protect her from the danger that was getting closer all the time?

"What do you think?" She turned her head just enough to whisper against his ear, her breath warm against the chill of his flesh. "Was this really an accident?"

He realized that she was seeking reassurance that the world wasn't as chaotic as she feared it to be.

Brian temporized. "It seems strange to me, but I suppose it could happen."

"The police can find out for sure, can't they, when they examine the body?"

"Yes," he said slowly, "if they examine the body."

"But why wouldn't they?" She moved away abruptly and gazed up into his face.

"Unless they know what's been going on, there is no reason to think it anything but an accident. Men are killed in the breaking ice every year. We are the only ones who knew Charlie was going to meet you and talk about Dimitri—and the official line is still that Dimitri's death was accidental."

"But we can tell them he was going to meet me—"

"I'm not sure that would be wise. They haven't listened to us up to now, have they? All they've been doing is trying to cover things up. And I have enough confidence in the police to believe that if they are covering something up they are under considerable pressure to do so from someone pretty high up. And anyone with that much clout isn't going to let them do much to discover what really happened here."

She stuck out her chin in that stubborn gesture he was beginning to know and dread. It meant more trouble for him.

"There must be something we can do to find out for

sure,'' she said. ''He might have talked to someone
here. If we could ask around—''

Gently, he turned her again until she fit into the
curve of his body, tightened his grip, and rested his
chin on the top of her head. She felt so natural in his
arms. ''I'm not sure we should do that. Asking around
seems to be dangerous for the people we ask.''

The Natives seemed to have made a decision. With
its macabre load, they pulled the sled in the direction
of the village. The knot of Natives broke up, straggling
away by twos and threes. Most followed toward the
village half a mile away.

They had nothing to say to Brian and Malinche; the
two would soon be alone. Alone with nothing accom-
plished. It was time to start back to town.

One woman hesitated, glancing first at the Natives
walking away, then back at Malinche and Brian. Then,
as though coming to a decision, she strode briskly toward them.

Even in her bulky clothes, she appeared slender and
graceful. As she drew closer, Brian noted that her face
was a delicate oval and her almond eyes, although
clouded with tears, shone with intelligence and determination.

''You are the ones who were friends with Charlie,''
she said.

Brian wanted the record kept straight. ''We really
didn't know him,'' he said. ''We hoped to see him
tonight. I'm terribly sorry we were too late.''

The woman gazed from one face to the other, as
though seeking an answer to a question she didn't ask.
Then she nodded, making up her mind. ''I'm Netta
Frank, Charlie's—wife. I would be honored if you
would come to our house. We can talk there.''

"His wife?" Malinche glanced at the sled laden with Charlie's body; it was almost to the village now, with its sorrowful escort.

The woman caught the glance. "His widow, now. They are taking him to the main lodge to arrange for burial. I should be with him. I will be soon. But there is something I must say to you first."

She turned without waiting for a reply and set off at a fast pace toward the village. Exchanging a glance, Brian and Malinche followed.

Her house was at the edge of the permanent settlement, and appeared to be a compromise between the regular houses and the tents of the nomads. Through a low door, she entered a small structure constructed of driftwood, stones and various types of animal bones, gesturing them to follow.

Brian surveyed the interior with interest. The inside was as primitive as the exterior. He had heard a few Natives still lived in this manner, eschewing as much as they could of civilization. With its walls covered with polar bear hides and with seal fur spread across the floor, the room was cozy and warm. Brian could easily believe they were back a century in time.

Netta Frank motioned them to a bench covered with a goose down cushion, and placed a teakettle on the oil stove—an obvious concession to "progress."

"I know," she said, with a rueful smile. "Charlie and I lived a little differently from some of the others. Charlie liked the old ways, although most of our people have adopted the ways of the white man. We're no longer nomadic, and we're on a money economy. We buy things rather than make them the way we used to do. But Charlie is—was different." She nearly choked, but continued. "He liked the traditional ways, and tried to follow them. I like them, too—although I insisted on a few things—tea among them.''

She reached for a square tin can and removed the lid. ''May I make you a cup?''

''Yes, thank you,'' Malinche said, keeping her tone as even as Netta's. She wasn't fooled by the surface placidity. The woman was obviously in shock, and clinging to the familiar to keep from breaking down entirely. They had to let her tell them her reasons for inviting them here in her own time. In the meantime, she would make conversation.

''How long were you and Charlie married?''

''Four years.'' The woman gave the teakettle her full and intense concentration, as though the familiar ritual could cast out demons.

''Any children?''

''No, not yet. I guess, not ever.''

It hadn't been a good choice for conversation. Malinche tried to think of something else to say.

''Where did you and Charlie meet?''

At this, Netta managed a genuine smile. ''You're thinking Kotzebue? Or maybe during the Eskimo Gathering? No, I was a teacher in Anchorage. Charlie brought some furs down for the Fur Rhondy.'' Seeing Malinche's puzzled expression, she explained, ''The Fur Rendezvous. It's held annually in Anchorage. It used to be the traders came to sell furs, but now its part festival. After that—it was fated. Although it took some time to get used to this.'' Her arm swung to indicate the small room. ''I insisted on some conveniences, so we compromised.''

Another person caught like herself between two cultures. Malinche emphasized with her dilemma. But Netta had made her choice, and had presumably been happy in it, while she, Malinche, twisted and turned like a weather vane, unable to settle in any one culture.

Guilt flooded her, as she watched Netta carefully make the tea. Yes, Netta had made a choice, and Malinche had taken it from her. By her dogged insistence on tracking Dimitri's killer, she had been responsible for Charlie's death.

Silence apparently didn't bother Netta. Perhaps she was deciding how to begin. They had sipped half a cup of hot green tea before Netta spoke.

"You saw the arguing down by the shore?"

"Yes," Malinche replied. "We wondered what it was about."

"There is some disagreement among the people about what to do about Charlie's death." She paused, swallowed, and went on. "Some want to call the authorities, others say that it was clearly an accident and we can handle it ourselves."

Brian's eyes narrowed. "What do you think?"

"Me?" Her voice trailed away; she gazed down at her hands, fighting for control, then took a deep breath and let it out explosively. "I do not believe it was an accident."

Although Brian agreed with her, he wanted to know her reasons for her conclusion. "Why not? I understand he was skilled in hunting, an expert with a kayak, but even a skilled person can misjudge, run into bad luck…"

"That's true. If it were only the accident, I might not be so sure. Charlie was skilled, but it's true any man can make a mistake. But to happen now—the timing is too much of a coincidence."

"Why?"

"I don't really have any facts—but something was

going on, something Charlie didn't want to tell me
about. He was excited when he came home today, but
frightened, too. He kept saying, he wondered if he was
doing the right thing, talking to you." She nodded at
Malinche. "But then he said he owed it to Dimitri."

"Did he say what he was going to tell us?"

"No. He said it was better if I didn't know—it might
be dangerous. That's why I think it wasn't an accident."

"Can't we find out for sure?" Malinche leaned forward and covered the woman's hand with hers. "An
autopsy would tell us...."

"No!" Netta's head jerked up. "I don't want him
cut up! Besides, what difference does it make if the
police confirm what we already know?"

"And even if the authorities confirm he was murdered, they won't necessarily tell us," Brian agreed.
"Look at the way they've covered up the truth about
Dimitri's death. And it looks like Charlie was murdered, too."

He rose and placed his mug on the table. "I'm very
sorry, Mrs. Frank. What can we do?"

"I want justice for Charlie," she said simply. "If he
was murdered, it must have had something to do with
what he was going to tell you. And the least I can do
for him is tell you as much as I know."

Netta's shoulders slumped and she jammed her fist
to her throat, pushing back sorrow. "But I'm afraid it's
not much."

"Just start at the beginning. Why did Charlie go to
Kotzebue today?"

"He usually went in, if he didn't plan on hunting.
And today he didn't intend to hunt—which makes it
even stranger that he should be out hunting in his

kayak. In town, he heard from several people about this woman who was asking questions about Dimitri. He didn't say he had arranged to meet you—just that he might talk to you about Dimitri.''

"Were he and Dimitri friends?''

Netta glanced at the table beside her where several ivory carvings rested in a row. "I don't think Charlie met him before he came here for the Gathering. But they became friends—they were both artists,'' she said with pride, her eyes filling with tears.

Brian and Malinche examined the carvings, waiting for Netta to regain control. Brian hadn't noticed the carvings before. They were finely done. Not in Dimitri's league, but beautiful.

Netta had wiped her eyes; her countenance was again composed, and Brian asked gently, "Did Dimitri usually come to the Gathering?''

Netta shook her head. "No, it was the first time. He was an Aleut, you know. He hadn't any relatives here. But he said he came this year looking for someone.''

"Who?'' Malinche leaned forward, her heart pounding with excitement. This might be the key to her search. Then Netta continued, and her heart fell.

"I don't know who he was looking for. Perhaps Charlie did. I overheard them talking about a letter Dimitri had written to the Department of the Army. He'd had a reply, and he was excited. I know he showed the letter to Charlie, but he never told me what it said.''

"Not even a hint?'' Malinche's eyes held Netta's, every muscle tense with hope. "Perhaps he mentioned something you might not have thought important. Anything?''

"No, I have no idea. It might have been a name,

because Dimitri was definitely looking for someone. I don't know who—but I think Charlie knew.''

Charlie knew. The words echoed, sinister and threatening. Malinche swallowed; her throat was suddenly dry. Dimitri had come to Kotzebue looking for someone, and Dimitri was dead. Charlie had known who he was looking for and now Charlie was dead.

Brian turned and reached for Malinche's hand. ''Thank you for talking to us, Mrs. Frank. I know it was hard for you.''

''Will it help?''

Her eyes held such mute, bottomless sorrow that Brian would have done anything he could to ease the pain, but it still seemed to him like a dead end. ''You gave us a lot of information we didn't have before. Let us know what's decided about the authorities.''

They left her staring sightlessly at nothing, a brave, stoic woman who postponed her grieving to do what she could for her husband. Brian suspected the minute the door closed behind them and she no longer had to keep up a facade she would collapse in grief.

''What do we do now?'' Malinche curled her fingers tightly around Brian's. She should have removed her hand, since she was resolved to keep things coolly friendly between them. And she would have—except that his hand felt so comforting, so warm. So right. As though her hand felt like it belonged within his. She was acutely aware of him standing beside her, a strong oak in a hurricane. She couldn't bear to break the contact.

''Let's talk,'' Brian said, glancing around the village. No one was outside, but he suspected everyone was watching and speculating as they left Netta's house. "Let's go someplace where we won't be overheard."

Whoever was dogging their trail was taking great care to make his victims' deaths appear accidental. It was only luck that Brian had found Dimitri before all evidence of foul play had been obliterated. And Charlie's body could just as easily have washed out to sea where he wouldn't have been found for months, if ever.

He took his backpack from the four-wheeler, and slung it over his shoulder, a habit so ingrained that he rarely ventured even a few yards into the bush without it. Many times the few supplies he carried had meant survival.

Without a clear destination, they walked toward the water. A few minutes later they stood on the shore of the Bering Strait, still holding hands. They were at the spot where Charlie's body had been taken from the ice, but Brian didn't dwell on that; you couldn't find a place where you would be less likely to be overheard.

Gazing out in the general direction of Siberia, Brian thought it didn't much matter which way he looked— the same flat, bleak landscape was all around them. Ice hugged the shore; a few feet farther out, the large chunks began to break into smaller pieces, leaving channels of blue water between huge floes.

At his feet the rocky shore blended almost imperceptibly with the icy sea. Behind him the land stretched monotonously, broken only occasionally by hillocks of low arctic shrubs. Half a mile away the village stood out darkly against the lighter tundra.

Aside from that, nothing indicated habitation; only a small shed about two hundred feet away broke the featureless landscape. He couldn't think of a better place to talk without being overheard.

But talking didn't seem half as urgent as kissing the lovely woman who stood beside him. Kissing her, holding her warm body, feeling her breasts against his chest with nothing between them. The desire was nearly overpowering. Forcing the thought away, he cleared his suddenly dry throat.

"Someone knew that Charlie intended to meet you," he said. "Did anyone overhear you when you talked to him this afternoon?

"I don't think so. Pasco and Wilson popped up often, but they weren't in the bar when I talked to Charlie. I don't think there was anyone else in the bar except the waitress." She hesitated, remembering.

"Yes? What about the waitress?"

"The woman tending bar was also the waitress. She brought my sandwich just as Charlie left. Or I thought she did. Actually, I have no idea how long she was standing there."

"So, you could have been overheard, or Charlie could have talked to someone. I suppose anyone could have known about the meeting."

"Maybe we could ask a casual question or two at the bar—"

"Hasn't the obvious occurred to you?" His tone was sharper than he meant it to be because he couldn't erase a feeling of guilt. By allowing Malinche to pursue this, he was implicated in Charlie's death. "Any time you start asking around, someone winds up dead. Innocent people."

His assessment stung. "Are you suggesting we forget about it? Let whoever killed my brother—and now Charlie—get away with it?"

He sighed. "I might be inclined to do just that. We're in way over our heads here. Netta seems like a nice woman. I'd hate for her to wind up dead just for talking to us. How do you weigh it? Keep nosing around and put more people in danger?'' He was talking to himself as much as to Malinche. ''Or do we just forget about Dimitri and accept the official version of his death? Which means the murderer goes unpunished.'' And still free to find us and silence us for good, he thought.

''Netta wanted to help. And you know very well if we don't do something, no one will,'' she said stubbornly.

''Yes, and I believe someone else knows that, too.'' He shrugged. ''I doubt the choice is ours any longer—hasn't been for quite a while. We could stop investigating, but how do we convince whoever is on our tail that we've stopped? We can hardly put an ad in the paper saying, 'I give up—you can forget about us now.'''

Actually, that wasn't entirely true. *He* probably could give up. His boss wanted him to cut and run, and he suspected if he washed his hands of the matter and went back to Anchorage he would be shipped out where he couldn't cause any more trouble.

But trouble to whom? What anonymous person was pulling his strings, had threatened his life? He was a man who minded his own business, but he had been pushed too far.

Brian had never considered himself hero material. He was a firm believer in the old adage: He who fights and runs away lives to fight another day.

But he couldn't leave Malinche to face things alone. Not now.

It could be that dragon, although he couldn't understand why it would pose a threat to anyone. It was like dozens of others Dimitri had made. He'd scrutinized it time and again and had seen nothing unusual. Or maybe she had picked up some information she didn't know she had. Whoever was trailing them would assume she had told him everything she knew. There seemed to be nothing to do but forge ahead. He just wished he knew what to do.

He had another reason for wishing he were not involved. But there was more than one danger. Malinche was growing on him, becoming necessary to him. He couldn't look at her without wanting her. This terrible, aching yearning, this longing to hold her, to kiss her, to feel her silky hair falling over his chest as it had done not so long ago in the cave, must be perfectly visible on his face. And every glance at her told him they were still from two different worlds.

She shivered, and he was immediately concerned. She had been sheltered all her life, shielded from storms. She was doing well, all things considered, but she was delicate, vulnerable. She should be cossetted, protected.

But not by me, he reminded himself. She had a Daddy for that.

"Let's get back to the hotel," he said. "There's nothing more we can do here. Maybe after a good night's sleep, something will occur to us."

He knew what would occur to him. Making love to her in a regular bed would be heaven.

A heaven he would pay for later.

"I keep thinking if we just keep trying we'll come up with a clue," she said. "It must be the letter."

They turned and walked back toward the village. Malinche kept slightly ahead. When they got back to the hotel, he was going to insist that she be more careful. He was going to ignore her stubborn resistance to suggestions, and see that she did as she was told. It might have been her as well as Charlie who "met with an accident." He would stick close by—certainly no hardship....

He glanced at the shed as they walked by it, absently, merely noting it was there.

Something shimmered in his subconscious, a faint, illusive uneasiness, but there seemed to be no reason for it. They were completely isolated. Nothing near them but the old abandoned shed, used for storing worn-out kayaks, leftover oil drums. There was no way he could have seen a flash of movement out of the corner of his eye—

A volcano exploded in his head. He staggered. Pain shattered him, fragmented him. He felt himself falling into a kaleidoscope of flames and fury.

He tried to fight it off, to climb back up, but the pain intensified. Then he was falling into an endless chasm of darkness.

Then nothing.

Chapter Ten

Unaware of the tears streaming down her cheeks, Malinche grasped Brian's shoulders and tried to turn him onto his back. He lay sprawled facedown on the ice. She saw with sickening clarity that his fair hair was matted with blood.

Was he dead? He couldn't be, he just couldn't!

Moving him terrified her. Any movement might start the blood flowing, but she had to see his face. She had to know if he still lived.

She couldn't turn him with the pack on is shoulders. She had to get it off, a seemingly impossible task in her panicked condition. Calm down, she ordered herself. She'd be no help to anyone this way. And she had to hurry; her fingers were becoming more numb by the second.

Finally, she located the buckles and unclasped them. Choking back a sob, she pulled the pack clear of his body. Now she could turn him. Pushing and pulling against his inert weight, she managed to position him so that she could see his face.

Her heart froze in her chest. She struggled against dizziness that threatened to envelop her. He was terribly pale, a translucent unnatural paleness, and his eyes remained shut. His lips were a cold faint blue, his mouth slightly open. If he lived it was by a thin thread.

Leaning over, she put her ear to his mouth. His breath came faintly, but it was there. Relief nearly swept her back into the darkness from which she had just emerged. Her weakness was quickly gone, replaced by grim determination. He was alive now, although future prospects didn't look good for either of them.

Ever since she had regained consciousness a few minutes ago, she had resolutely kept her eyes and her thoughts only on Brian. It was the only way to control her panic. How they came to be on an ice sheet out in the open water, she had no idea, but that was certainly where they were.

She shook him again, more forcefully. It might cause the blood to flow again, but he couldn't just lie there, waiting to freeze to death. She wouldn't allow him to leave her alone!

Nothing. No response at all. She gave up and covered her face with her hands. Hunched over on the ice, she tried to shield herself from the wind that poked and twisted at her back, seeking a way through her down parka. Even though she was warmly dressed and the sun still circled above the horizon, she was cold.

There had to be a way out of this mess. Brian had to move....

As though she willed it, a low moan escaped his mouth. She stared at his face, hope mingling with trepidation. He still hadn't opened his eyes, but he seemed to be regaining consciousness. His gloved hand dug into the ice, as though searching for something.

She grasped his hand and squeezed tightly. "Brian! Brian! Wake up! Please, wake up!"

He groaned again, and his eyes slowly opened.

With a cry, she knelt and cradled his head on her knees. He stared up at her, bewildered.

"Malinche?"

"Yes, it's me. Are you all right?"

He tried to smile, but it was a weak effort. "All right? It doesn't feel much like it. What happened?"

"We'll talk in a minute. Can you sit up?"

He struggled to a sitting position, rubbing his head. "I feel like I came out on the losing end of a fight with a grizzly. What happened?" Still rubbing his head, he glanced away from her and stiffened. "And where the hell are we?"

Malinche gazed across the ice-choked water, which she had been trying not to do ever since she regained consciousness on this miserable floating chunk of ice. As far as she could determine, they were well offshore; all around her ice floes churned and rocked, performing a mad ballet. The noise was horrendous as ice ground against ice, sometimes breaking in the process, sometimes slipping away to leave chasms of ice blue water between.

"Where are we?" she repeated in a small voice. "How about between the devil and the deep blue sea."

"Very funny," he growled. He started to struggle to his feet, but the chunk of ice swayed precariously and he sank back down. "Are you all right?"

"I suppose so. I came to before you did, and I don't have a headache. But I don't have a clue as to how we got here."

He shook his head. "Let's try to reconstruct it. The last thing I remember, I was walking away from the shore toward the village. You were slightly in front— that's all I remember."

"We were walking by an old shed," she said. "I

heard something—a thud, a grunt—and I turned. Just as something hit me over the head. I didn't know a thing until I woke up. You were lying there on the ice—you were so still." She swallowed, remembering her fear. "I thought you were dead."

And I was scared to death. Not just because I might be alone on a chunk of ice floating God knows where, but scared that you might be gone. I couldn't bear it if anything happened to you.

"Well, I'm not dead." He rubbed his head, then scanned the blood clinging to his fingers. "So, somebody hit us over the head. How could I have been so stupid? I was so careful to get away from everybody so no one would overhear us, and I walked right by that shed—where anyone could be hiding."

"It wasn't your fault. It seemed to be abandoned—"

"And I thought I saw a flash of movement out of the corner of my eye. I should have moved quicker—"

"There was nothing you could have done. There's no reason to berate yourself. But what did he accomplish by marooning us out here?"

Brian gazed out over the sea, a sinking feeling in his chest. The surface of the water was heaving and tossing with chunks of ice for as far as he could see. The pattern appeared random, but he knew it wasn't. A light wind combined with the tide to push the ice in one direction. Horrified, he saw that although individual chunks spun and turned, the field of broken ice was drifting out into the open sea—including the island they were on.

He didn't want to alarm Malinche, but she was no fool; she undoubtedly recognized the danger. "I think that whoever has been on our trail thinks he's found a way of getting rid of us permanently.''

"Maybe he has."

She looked so very small huddled into her parka, and his heart ached for her. He would get her out of this situation; he had to. "This is no time to give up. We'll think of something."

He glanced around their floating ice pad. It was discouragingly small—not over twenty by fifteen feet. Any collision might break it in two. As it was, it felt unstable, rocking and jolting as though it might capsize any minute.

He reached for his blue canvas pack, lying in stark contrast against the white. "At least he left my backpack. I wonder why he did that?"

"Maybe it was just too cumbersome to get off. He had to work fast to knock us both out and carry us out on this ice."

"He probably had a boat or a snowmobile stashed in that shed," Brian said. "He must be getting desperate. It took a lot of nerve to bring us out into this ice field."

"Brian—are we going to die?" Malinche whispered.

Her words galvanized him. He would get her out of this, he swore he would.

He didn't see exactly how, though. The ice chunk they were on would only last so long. It could capsize any minute. If it somehow managed to remain intact, it would continue its drift into the open water. Somehow they had to get off it and onto a larger chunk. It would at least buy them time.

Simple to say; it seemed impossible to do. He surveyed the chasm between them and the nearest stable ice sheet. The distance was well over twenty feet—no way could they jump it. Tiny particles of ice floated in the black water like frosty stars in a black night sky. Trying to swim across would mean immediate death from freezing. And if the ice sheet came closer, the risk was even greater. The behemoth might slide right over their small chunk and demolish it—along with them.

There was one chance, a small one, but it was all he could think of. Anything was better than just sitting here waiting.

He unzipped his backpack and took out a geologist's hatchet. A small roll of light nylon cord came from another pocket. Quickly, he tied the cord to the hatchet.

"You do come prepared," Malinche said. "Were you ever a Boy Scout? And what on earth do you intend to do with that?"

At least she could still joke. He grinned, trying to appear confident and in charge. His plan had one chance in a thousand of success. "No, I was never a Boy Scout, but they would take away my geologist's license if I ever went anywhere without a hatchet and a rope."

He had better hurry. Malinche's face was pinched with cold and she was shivering. Although she was warmly dressed, her clothes couldn't keep out the bitter cold forever. Although he was used to weather extremes, he felt it, too, the numbness that slowed his reflexes, stiffened his joints.

She struggled to her feet, swaying to keep her balance, as the ice chunk dipped with the current. "Whatever you're going to do, you'd better do it. This floating ice cube isn't going to last much longer."

As though to lend credence to her words, a chunk broke off a corner and plunged into the water, sending icy spray upward. Worse still, the chasm between their ice and the largest ice sheet was steadily widening as they drifted farther out to sea.

He couldn't wait. He stood, bracing his legs, and hurled the hatchet at the nearest large ice sheet.

It plunged into the water, only a few feet from the target. Swearing, he pulled the rope back and retrieved the hatchet. He had to make it in his next two or three tries. The cold and his injury combined to sap his strength.

Again he braced himself and threw the hatchet. It was closer this time, grazing the shelf of ice, but not close enough. It fell into the sea.

He pulled it back and stood for a moment, gathering his strength. Malinche stood silently beside him. If strength of will could help him, he knew she was assisting him with every throw. If they didn't drift any farther, if the large ice sheet remained stable, if—

He wondered how much blood he had lost before the cold congealed the flow. Enough to make him weak in the knees, at least. He took a deep breath, summoning all his determination. If he didn't make it this time he doubted he would have the strength to try again.

He drew back his arm and hurled the hatchet with all of his power and some reserve he didn't know he had. So much depended on this; it had to catch. He closed his eyes, willing the hatchet to find its target.

"You did it, you did it!"

At Malinche's shout, he opened his eyes. The hatchet was buried in the immense ice sheet.

Relief washed over him in a wave so strong his legs nearly buckled. They had a chance. Just a chance, but it was better than nothing.

Tentatively, he tugged at the nylon cord. The hatchet

remained buried in the ice. He pulled harder; it didn't budge.

"What now?"

"Now we try to pull ourselves over to that ice sheet." He dug his heels into the ice and wrapped the cord around his arm. Malinche grabbed the line and braced her boots in the ice.

"Pull!"

They pulled on the line, every muscle straining, as they tried to close the distance between themselves and the larger ice sheet.

"It's not moving! Pull!"

"I am!" Malinche gasped.

The line remained taut, but nothing moved. A few minutes later, they collapsed on the ice, exhausted. The distance between the two ice sheets remained the same.

"We're not going to make it," Malinche said.

Inside, Brian agreed, but they were still alive. There was hope. "We're not as bad off as we were," he replied. "We can't pull ourselves closer—but we're not drifting farther away, either. We've gained some time."

"If this chunk doesn't break up."

"If it does, we'll use the cord to pull ourselves over to the other sheet."

She gave him a half smile, showing her gratitude that he was trying to keep up her spirits even if he was insulting her intelligence. Immersion in that icy water wasn't an option, and they both knew it. Even if they made it across they would freeze in a few minutes, dying of exposure.

Malinche had never been so close to dying. Even in the cave she had always believed they would be rescued, or they would find their own way to safety. And the cave had been relatively comfortable; they had been warm, had plenty to eat. In fact, she looked back on the days in the cave with affection. She had known some of the most beautiful moments of her life there.

The nearness of death was said to clarify the mind. If she had to die, she wanted to be as close as she could to Brian. She felt that was where she was meant to be. Where she belonged, even in death. The force of that insight was stronger than her fear.

She watched him tie the rope around his arm and take a sweater from his backpack. Spreading it on the ice, he sat down and pulled her into his lap. She snuggled against him, feeling his arms tighten around her. She wondered how long they could last, but the thought didn't bring terror, only sadness.

His nearness gave her strength. She shook off her bleak mood; she wouldn't give in to despair. They could last several hours and anything could happen.

"That backpack of yours is a wonder," she murmured. "You don't happen to have any food in there, do you?"

He pulled her closer, holding his cheek against hers. "A few days fasting won't hurt you. I'm told thin is in."

"You're not implying I'm fat?" She rubbed her lips softly against his cheek.

"Offhand, I'd say you're perfect."

They chattered on, both knowing their words made little sense. It served though, to hold back the sense of powerlessness, as they rocked gently in the middle of the ice field, with nothing on the horizon but more ice.

"What were you like as a little boy?" she asked.

"Well, I was alone a lot, but I was lucky. There was a creek to play in and frogs to catch. My father probably never actually realized he had a child, or if he did, he didn't give it much thought. My mother had other priorities. No one bothered me if I stayed out late. Sometimes I spent all night on the creek bank, nestled in the grass, looking up at the stars. That's where I learned to love nature, to trust it.''

As I never trusted people. And I still don't. The closer you get to my heart, Malinche, the worse it will be when we get out of here, and you leave. If, of course, we actually get out.

''What about your childhood?''

''Idyllic,'' she said. ''I didn't have a mother, and I missed her, but I belonged to the entire village. I had an absolute sense of security. When my dad took me to Seattle and dressed me up and sent me to private schools, I felt like I'd been dumped in ice water. That's when I really began to miss her, to understand what I'd missed. Her absence left a big hole in my heart I couldn't fill. I decided to come up here to search for who she was, and to find a missing part of myself.''

A floating chunk of ice rammed into the one they were on.

''If this thing takes another bump like that,'' Brian said, ''we'll both be dumped in ice water.''

The cold was seeping into his bones. He was still dizzy from the blow to his head; he wasn't sure he was capable of thinking straight. The only good thing he could see about their situation was that they remained closer to the larger ice sheet, which in turn remained closer to shore. But for how long?

He tightened his arms around Malinche; in response she pressed closer. Tenderness nearly overwhelmed him, as he placed a feathery kiss on the top of her head. This couldn't be the end of everything. Not when he had finally realized how much he loved this woman, how precious she was—

The thought had sneaked up on him, surprising him with its intensity. Yes, he admitted to himself. He did love her. And he would do anything humanly possible to protect her. Right now, that didn't seem to be much.

Loving her didn't change anything, except to make his heart heavier. It didn't make it easier to rescue her. But he would do it, he vowed. He would see her safely to land. As for the future...

He wouldn't think of that now. There would be no future of any kind if they didn't survive. And whatever happened, he wanted her to be safe and happy.

"I still wonder why he didn't take my backpack," he mused. "Apparently he didn't take anything..."

Malinche's hand went to her throat. She had grown accustomed to the gold chain around her neck, the jade dragon between her breasts. Something had nagged at her ever since she regained consciousness, a sense of something missing, but she had been so bundled up she hadn't noticed—

Her hand closed over emptiness. "Brian. The dragon—it's gone."

"That's what he wanted," Brian said grimly. "My pack, nothing else mattered. He got what he wanted, and then stranded us out here on the ice where he expected us to die."

Malinche stuck her hand in her pocket, and withdrew it empty. "That's not all he took," she said quietly. "The envelope is gone, too."

"So, he took every clue we had," Brian said, "and then left us to die."

"Why didn't he just kill us there? Why go to all this trouble?"

"Because he has to make it look like an accident," Brian said. "So far, his attempts to make his murders seem like accidents have more or less succeeded. We're the only ones who won't let it drop. He's been able to apply pressure somehow—even the police won't get involved. But it would be different with us. We're not Natives, who might be expected to be killed in some dangerous pursuit. We're not powerless. Your father is a man with influence. If you were murdered, you can bet your soul he'd turn up the heat."

"While if I died in an accident, he'd accept it."

"Right. And my employers wouldn't stand still for murder either—"

He broke off. Was that true? What would his company do if he was murdered? He wasn't sure anymore. They were involved at some level. An accident might be in their best interests, also.

"If we do get out of here alive," Malinche said, "maybe he'll leave us alone. Now that he's got everything he wanted."

"Maybe." Brian doubted it. Their attacker could never be sure how much they knew; he wouldn't have left them to die on the ice if all he wanted was the dragon and the envelope.

But now wasn't the time for speculation. Their situation was becoming more perilous by the minute. They were drifting closer to the larger ice floe, but bits and pieces were breaking off of their own. At the rate the chunk was disintegrating, Brian calculated only a few minutes remained.

The chunk was lighter now, easier to manipulate. That was one thing in their favor. Then, too, a momentary shift in the current halted the relentless push out to sea. Perhaps with the shift in the current, the lightness of the chunk of ice that supported them, another try might be successful.

"Up you go," he said, pushing Malinche up from his lap. She staggered a bit; her legs were probably as numb as his own, but at least she stood. He rose to his feet, pleasantly surprised to find he was able to stand. They couldn't delay any longer.

Again he dug in his heels and pulled on the nylon cord. The hatchet held firm in the ice, but there was still a good fifteen feet between the two ice sheets. "Pull!"

Malinche needed no urging. Every ounce of strength and will focused on that thin nylon cord and the ice sheet so near and yet so far away. Inch by imperceptible inch, it drew closer. Now only ten or twelve feet separated them from relative safety.

Her arms felt as though they were being pulled from the sockets. In spite of the cold, sweat sprang out on her face. Brian grunted and gasped, as his shoulders bulged with the effort. But they were moving. Now only eight or ten feet remained...

But she couldn't go on. She couldn't continue the pressure. Her arms were limp, her legs like mush. She had given all she had....

"Now!" Brian shouted. "Pull!"

From some reserve deep inside her, adrenaline surged. They were within five feet of the large sheet, but they could get no closer.

She sobbed with frustration. So close, yet so impossible to bridge.

"We'll have to jump," Brian said.

Sheer terror gripped Malinche, as she stared down into the water seething with slushy ice. Jump, he said. A five-foot jump from a bobbing cork to an ice sheet that heaved and ground with the pressure of breaking up. She could never make it.

"Hurry up. There's not much time."

"You first!"

"No. You can do it. I know you can. Now, go!"

He knew a lot more than she did, then. But she had to try. She backed away a couple of feet to get a running start, then launched herself across the chasm, knowing she'd never make it.

Brian's hands cupped her bottom and propelled her across like a volleyball. She sprawled on the ice, gasping, safe by at least three feet. A thought flashed through her mind. This was once she didn't mind Brian telling her what to do.

But the momentum of her jump had shoved the ice chunk still farther away. She watched, not daring to breathe. What good would it do for her to be here on this sheet of ice if Brian was marooned on the other? She couldn't let that happen.

She sprang up and began pulling on the cord that still united the two ice floes. Desperation gave her renewed strength. The chunks inched closer. Then Malinche held her breath as Brian took a running leap.

Everything seemed to happen in slow, agonizing motion. She saw his boots leave the ice chunk, saw him float across the space between them, just as the ice he had been on splintered into a dozen pieces. An eternity later, he landed on the ice beside her.

She hurled herself into his arms, and they fell gasping on the ice. For endless moments, neither had the breath to say a word.

Finally, still speechless, they struggled to their feet and surveyed their situation. It could have been worse, Brian thought. At least they wouldn't drift out to sea, or drown. Of course they might very well freeze to death. How long could anyone survive in this weather without food or shelter?

As though she knew what was on his mind, Malinche spoke softly. "How long do you think we've been out here?"

He glanced at his watch, then up at the sky. "It's nearly midnight. We've been here several hours at least. But I've heard of people existing for days under conditions like these."

"Will somebody miss us and start searching?"

He shrugged. "Maybe. But I didn't tell the man I rented the four-wheeler from how long I'd be gone. Besides, where would they search?"

He had a point, Malinche admitted to herself. The ice sheet stretched all along the coastline. For as far as she could see, nothing existed but sheets of ice broken in spots by blue-black water. If anyone from the land did happen to notice two black specks on the ice, they would probably think they were seals. They might be spotted from the air, but George and his plane had gone back to Barrow, and no one else would be looking for them.

"We could walk toward shore," she suggested. "Maybe this part of the ice field is connected to land."

Brian nodded and retrieved his hatchet and cord. "At least moving will keep us warm."

They began walking around the perimeter of the ice sheet. It was slow going, like walking across a field of lava spewed by an insane volcano. Only this volcano hadn't sent forth molten lava; it had erupted with boulders of ice. They were trapped in an eerie moonscape of treacherous crevasses and sharp spires.

Still they slogged along; there was nothing else to

do. The sun pointed out the general direction and if their strength held out they just might survive. Besides, staying still was an invitation to freeze to death.

It was impossible to tell how far they had gone, but Malinche felt that she had been moving forever. Her universe had shrunk to putting one foot in front of the other. She walked behind Brian, focusing on his broad back. To look around would be to invite despair.

He halted, and she nearly ran into him.

"What is it?"

"We've gone this way as far as we can."

She peeked around his body, and her heart sank even further. This ice sheet was large, but it was still an island. Separating it from another ice sheet was a long, jagged crack through which Malinche could see the ice blue of open water. Again their route had been cut off.

"Can we jump it like we did the other?"

He shook his head. "Not here. It may narrow a little farther along."

They trailed along the edge of the ice sheet, their pace slower as exhaustion set in. But as Brian had hoped, they finally reached a channel that might be narrow enough to cross. Or they could have crossed it, had they the energy and strength they had a few hours ago. Now, although the crack was only about four feet wide, it looked daunting.

Poised on the edge, Malinche stared down into the water. If she did fall in, wouldn't it be preferable to this agony? Her legs were numb, her face had lost all feeling. It would be quick. No one could survive in that water for more than a few minutes.

Brian grabbed her arm. "Stop that! Stop that right now!"

"How did you know what I was thinking?"

His lips appeared painfully chapped, but he still managed a grin. "You can't fool me. And you're not a quitter. Now, jump!"

Her rebellious legs obeyed one more time. Whether they would again, she doubted. But she was safe for now on the other side. Brian jumped and landed right beside her. Whether they had gained anything, she doubted also. The new ice field stretched out into the bleak distance.

"Come on." Brian took her hand, and she stumbled along beside him. His will alone kept her going. His will and the intense feeling she had for him. She couldn't tell whether they were making headway, but her legs kept moving.

With an inarticulate cry, she fell to her knees, unable to move another step. "I have to rest a minute."

Brian nodded, and knelt beside her, cradling her in his arms. Her thoughts made no sense. She knew she was approaching delirium. That might account for the thought. If she had to die here in this bleak nothingness, dying in Brian's arms would ease the pain. Make it bearable.

Brian held her as close as he could, hoping to transfer some heat to her body. Not that he had much heat to transfer. His very bones felt frozen. He calculated they had been on the ice for nearly twenty hours. They were close to the end of their endurance.

He wondered if they would ever be found. This ice would break up and drift out to sea, finally vanishing as it reached warmer water. If they were still on it, they, too, would vanish.

Holding her shivering body as though it were a lifeline, he admitted what he had known since he had first seen her. He loved her. And it wasn't only physical desire. He loved everything about her, her beauty, her compassion, her courage, her intelligence.

Had they managed to get safely off this ice sheet, he doubted he would ever have told her. But things had changed. These were the last hours, perhaps moments, they would ever have. And he needed desperately to tell her he loved her. He had to say the words, see her face when he acknowledged the love that had been growing since she had knocked on his apartment door.

And perhaps, if God was good, Malinche would whisper the words back to him.

It wasn't the most auspicious time or place for a declaration of love. There should be soft breezes and flowers, maybe moonlight. There should be a future....

He bent over her and kissed her cold lips. "Malinche, I—"

She tensed in his arms. "Do you hear that?"

He heard something; was it his heart pounding in his ears?

It came faintly across the ice, sharp yips, staccato barks. There was no mistaking it now.

With the last of his strength, he pulled her to her feet. He could hardly believe what he saw. Across the ice, a black line weaving through the uneven icescape, came a team of dogs.

Chapter Eleven

Malinche lay still, not daring to open her eyes, as she tried to get her bearings. Where was she, and what had awakened her? Warmth permeated her body, blessed warmth infiltrating the bone-breaking cold that had been her universe. Instead of the sound of ice crunching and howling around her, she heard the soft murmur of voices.

She pushed back a rising tide of panic. Was this the way it ended? She had heard that just before you freeze to death, a soft languorous heat comes over you, and you feel comfortable, even euphoric.

She forced herself to concentrate. She had been near freezing to death when she had seen the dogsled speeding across the ice field. After that, she didn't remember a thing.

If she opened her eyes, the warmth and tranquillity might vanish. Yet she *had* seen the sled coming. Had it been rescue or someone arriving to finish what he had started?

"I think she's coming around."

The voice was unfamiliar, but not threatening. She opened her eyes. At first she didn't know where she was, except that she was in a narrow bed snuggled under a fur covering. The room seemed full of people, all crowding around and looking down at her with anxious eyes. She struggled to sit up.

"Don't move. Rest awhile. You had a rough time." She recognized Brian, as he eased her back on the bed with gentle hands.

Brian. A glow of pure joy suffused her. He was here and everything was all right. Although *he* certainly didn't look all right, she thought, sinking back down on her pillow. Lines of worry bracketed his mouth; exhaustion showed in his eyes. A large bandage covered his hair. A tenderness so exquisite it was almost pain pierced her heart. She longed to smooth the worry from his face, kiss the exhaustion away.

A woman stepped up to him and eased him back down on a chair. "We'll take care of her. You won't help by collapsing yourself. You haven't rested at all."

The voice was soft, reassuring, and Malinche tore her gaze from Brian. "Netta." Again she struggled to rise. "What happened? What are we doing here?"

"Shhh. You need something to eat."

Food had been the last thing on her mind when she awoke, but at the mention of it she was ravenous. There were so many questions, but the steam from the broth Netta was ladling into a bowl drove them all from her mind.

Strong hands positioned her against the pillow; she accepted the bowl and raised it to her lips. It tasted better than anything she had ever eaten in her life; she gulped it like a savage.

Netta nodded with satisfaction, then took another bowl to Brian. "Here. You were too worried to eat before." He hesitated, and Netta patted his shoulder.

''She's going to be all right. I think you willed her to recover. Drink this—it will keep up your strength.''

Her hunger partially assuaged, Malinche sipped slowly and looked around the room. She was on a cot in Netta's small living area, the same room she had visited what now seemed like ages ago. The stove poured out heat, the array of carvings still sat on a shelf near the table. The carvings reminded her; her hand fluttered to her throat, bare now of her jade talisman.

She surveyed the other people; there weren't as many as she had originally thought. The small size of the room had given her that impression. Even the four other people in it—Netta, Brian, and two men she didn't know, seemed a crowd.

''She will be all right. Her spirit has returned.''

Malinche glanced at the speaker who was squatting on a stool in a corner, half hidden in shadows. He was extremely old, with a face the color of worn leather wrinkled with exposure to the elements. Age had honed away all excess flesh and he looked as fragile as the feather of an arctic tern. His eyes, though, black and alert, belied any infirmity. His gaze was so compelling that once meeting it, she found it difficult to glance away.

''This is Ganook,'' Netta said, in answer to Malinche's unspoken question. ''He is a great healer. We sent for him when Tommy arrived from the ice field with you both.''

The other man, apparently Tommy, nodded. It was difficult to tell his age, but Malinche guessed he was in his middle thirties. In the overheated room, he wore only a shirt, denim pants, and fur mukluks, but spread over a chair were a heavy fur parka and leather leggings.

"How long have we been here?"

Brian bent toward her and smoothed her hair back from her face as though caressing a rare treasure. The touch was infinitely tender. "Several hours," he said. "You've been a regular sleepyhead."

"Please. Tell me what happened."

Brian glanced at the old man, who nodded. "You conked out on me just as Tommy here arrived in his sled. We loaded you on and brought you here," he said. "That's just about it."

Just about it! They had been in the middle of a heaving field of ice with crevasses opening all around them. "How did he get across the cracks in the ice?"

Tommy grinned. "You tourists shouldn't wander around where you don't know what you're doing."

"Hey," Brian said, smiling. "I should resent that, but I don't feel like quibbling with our rescuer."

"It wasn't that easy," Tommy admitted. "We're used to traveling on the ice field, finding spots where we can cross, but there were times I wasn't all that sure myself. But I figured you had to be out there so I kept going."

"How did you figure that?" Malinche handed her bowl to Netta who refilled it and brought it back. "I didn't think anyone knew we were there."

"You had to be somewhere around here," Tommy said. "Your four-wheeler was still parked outside. At first we didn't worry about it—figured you were in somebody's house or even, knowing how crazy you whites are, you might just be walking around. But when the four-wheeler was still there, several hours later, we thought we'd better look around."

Netta nodded, picking up the story. "We asked everybody if they'd seen you. You weren't in any of the houses. The last anybody remembered seeing you was when you were walking toward the shoreline.''

"You weren't inside a house, you weren't on the shore,'' Tommy said. "Only one place you could be—on the ice. Though I couldn't think of anybody dumb enough to do that.''

"We didn't exactly go of our own accord,'' Brian said, fingering the bandage on his head.

"Yeah, we finally figured that out,'' Tommy replied.

"No more than Charlie was out hunting seals alone,'' Netta murmured.

Brian's grip tightened on Malinche's hand, and she suspected he was thinking the same thing she was. They had come very close to meeting Charlie's fate. She gazed up at him, feeling his concern pour over her like warm honey. His love? For one minute out there on the ice, she had thought he was about to tell her he loved her. Probably it had been a hallucination, brought on by cold and fear and hunger—and wishful thinking.

Ganook spoke again, a soft whisper that seemed to come from far away. His eyes looked into a distance invisible to the others. "There is evil out there. Strong evil. I have felt it for many moons. I felt it gathering around the artist who brings dragons to life. Then around the best hunter in the village. Now, the two of you. You must be constantly on guard. The evil is strong.'' He took a small pouch from somewhere in his clothes and handed it to her. "Keep this with you—it may help.''

Drawn by the power in his words, Malinche gave him her full attention. He seemed to belong to another age; she had seen no one like him among the Natives she knew, almost all of whom dressed in Western clothes, had Western names. Ganook made all that influence seem a passing fad. He remained the real voice of the people, their soul, never silenced though often ignored.

Something stirred inside Malinche, something basic and ageless. Her spine prickled, her hair rose on the back of her neck. Men and women like Ganook had led the people since time began, healing, prophesying, guarding. Shamans were said to commune with the spirits, to travel under the earth and to the moon, and into the hearts of people. She had never believed that—or had she? Was this what she was searching for?

Old myths she had forgotten returned to her, myths told to her by the people of the village where she had lived until she was seven. She clutched the pouch tightly in her hand. At the moment she didn't doubt this old man knew what he was talking about. "Sir—do you know where the evil lives. Who it is?"

He gave her a benign smile. "No. But great danger surrounds you and the young man."

"We figured that," Brian said dryly. "It doesn't take magic to figure it out, not when your plane's been tampered with, you've been shot at, and attacked and left on the ice." Obviously, he wasn't as impressed as she was with the shaman's manner and words. "Someone must have been hiding in that shed and hit us over the head when we walked by."

"We thought the same," Netta said, "so we looked around. We saw snowmobile tracks, and no one in the village had been near it for weeks."

"Someone must have seen him," Brian insisted.

Tommy shrugged. "There was a big crowd down on the shore when we found Charlie. Most people had parkas on. It would be easy enough to pull the fur over your face, disguise yourself, especially since we had our minds on other things.''

''Then he could have been right there in the crowd.''

''A stranger was there,'' Ganook agreed.

All heads swung toward him. He seemed only half attentive, his eyes fixed on some object none of them could see.

''How do you know?'' Brian demanded.

Ganook smiled. ''Oh, the information didn't come from the spirit world. I noticed him because I had seen him before. I glanced at his face, by chance, really. Even though he was all bundled up, wearing our Native garb, I remembered I had seen him before. At the Eskimo Gathering.''

Brian sucked in his breath. ''What did he look like?''

Ganook ignored the question, intent on telling his story in his own way. ''The one stranger I had seen before—the other was new to me.''

''There were two strangers!''

Again Ganook ignored him. ''The one I had seen before wasn't tall and he wasn't young, but he was powerfully built. Hard blue eyes, a harsh mouth, jaw like a rock. The other was tall, but slimmer, and his eyes showed nothing.''

''The first sounds like a good description of Carl Bettnor,'' Brian said, ''but I can't think of who could have been with him.''

''I didn't say they were together,'' Ganook replied, a slight reproof in his voice. ''In fact, I got the impression that the slim man would rather not be seen by the first. An impression only.''

Brian sighed, dropping his head into his hands. ''I don't think we've any choice now. We're going to have to go to the police. About what happened to us, and about Charlie.''

The three Natives bowed their heads in acquiescence.

BRIAN GLANCED DOWN at Malinche striding along beside him. They'd been back in Kotzebue only a couple of hours, but she'd bounced back marvelously from her ordeal on the ice. She seemed to have recovered physically, but he wondered how long it would take to erase the terror from her heart. She was so impossibly dear to him. His throat tightened, as he watched the wind sweep her dark hair away from her face and bring a hint of color to her deep ivory skin.

Her beauty tore at his heart. But then, he had known she was beautiful from the first minute he saw her. Now he knew she was courageous, intelligent, compassionate.

And determined. She had wanted to involve the police when Charlie had been killed, and he hoped she wasn't going to be disappointed now. He didn't want her to ever be disappointed or unhappy or—most importantly—ever in danger again.

The police station was only a block from the hotel and they had decided to walk, even though the wind was warning of an imminent storm. In spite of the cold, sweat sprang out on his face. If the storm had burst upon them while they were stranded on the ice, they would have had no chance at all. Not even Tommy's skill could have saved them.

Yet was that the entire reason he hesitated to commit himself to her? Perhaps she could overcome the hardships. She had certainly done better than he had expected. But could he bear the guilt of taking her from her privileged life. Was he egotistical enough to think their love would be worth it? And how it would hurt if she did run home to "Daddy."

And if they hadn't been rescued just at that time, he would have told her that he loved her.

Was that the reason he was drenched with sweat? Not the closeness of their escape from death, but his escape from commitment? And he truly wasn't sure which escape he was most grateful for. Not that he didn't love her. That was precisely the problem. He couldn't deny any longer that he loved her with all his heart. His soul. Every fiber of his being.

But if he had actually said the words, and she had responded, he would have been lost. He was a realist and he knew she could never be happy in his world. Oh, she had managed well so far, had gone through incredible hardship without complaint, but that had been forced on her.

But what would happen when she had a choice? His world was harsh and lonely, no place for a delicate beautiful woman. No woman could be expected to put up with the hardships, the lack of social amenities, the rigors of a geologist's life. By definition, they inhabited the lonely places of the earth. His stays in Anchorage were short, his times in the field long. She was tough, resilient, he had to admit it. But she'd had no choice. And there would always be Daddy to the rescue.

An hour later they returned to the hotel. Looking at Malinche's despondent face, Brian took no joy in the fact that he had been vindicated. The sheriff had listened politely, but said there was nothing he could do. The Eskimo, Charlie, had clearly died from an accident. Malinche and Brian had no clue as to who had abducted them, so what could he do?

They climbed the stairs slowly to their rooms.

Malinche seemed near collapse. "Do you think some-one is pressuring him?" she asked.

"I don't know. Our story might sound pretty thin to someone who didn't know all the facts."

By unspoken agreement, they went to Brian's room. Even walking along the corridor, Malinche found her-self glancing at the closed doors, wondering if someone waited within. Would she ever regain the nerve to stay alone? Not until this thing was resolved, at least.

He unlocked the door and she entered ahead of him, her hand straying to her neck where the dragon, now missing, had hung.

She flung herself down in the room's one comfort-able chair. "I think the dragon must be the key, though I can't understand how. Dimitri must have made hun-dreds of the things."

Brian didn't reply. He stretched out on the bed, eyes closed. With a wrench, she realized how exhausted he must be. The bed wasn't made for a tall man; his feet hung over the edge.

At the ridiculous sight, a surge of tenderness brought tears to her eyes. He looked so vulnerable, so young, with dark shadows under his eyes, his skin still pale from loss of blood. His injury had been much worse than hers, and yet he had watched over her all the while she slept at Netta's.

It must mean something. It must mean he cared for her. She couldn't be imagining that out on the ice, just before they were rescued, he was about to tell her so. But maybe she had willed it so strongly that she had heard what he hadn't said.

She rose and went to sit beside him on the bed, gently pushing his hair back from his face, and bending down to kiss his lips. He murmured something, but didn't awake.

Why wonder and speculate, when she could just ask him? Force the issue. It was time she knew where she stood. Those days were long gone when a woman waited passively for a man to declare his feelings.

She wasn't sure when her own had changed so drastically, when she had come to trust him so completely. As for his macho need to be in command—without his decisiveness, his firm will, they wouldn't have made it off the ice. Yes, she knew her own feelings; she loved him. But could he love her the way she needed to be loved?

He didn't open his eyes. His deep, even breathing told her he was asleep. She drew the comforter from the foot of the bed and placed it gently over his lean body. Then she slipped off her shoes and cuddled in beside him. She would lie here, safe and protected, until he woke. Then they would talk—before or after they made love....

She needed him now, needed to envelop him in herself, needed to feel his passion that set her own desire blazing. Needed to know it wasn't temporary...

In his sleep, he turned toward her, drawing her into the curve of his long body. One hand found her breast, closed around it. Blissfully, she relaxed against him. In less than a minute, she, too, was asleep.

From somewhere far away came a determined pounding. *Thud. Thud. Thud.* She struggled up out of a deep sleep trailing fragments of darkness and dreams. She flung one arm out to where Brian had been lying.

Nothing. She jerked instantly awake, heart pounding, and glanced frantically around the room. Then she relaxed; he was standing at the door.

"Okay, okay. Don't break it down." He opened the door. Joe Pasco practically fell into the room.

"Brian! I just heard. Are you two all right?"

"Yeah, we're okay." Brian's hand sought the back of his head. "Took a bit of a bump on the head, but nothing serious."

"That's not what I heard. It sounded serious to me. Another hour or so and the two of you would have been dead." He glanced at Malinche. "How is she?"

"I can speak for myself—I'm fine." Malinche sat up and smoothed her jeans over his hips. She knew Pasco resented her, possibly because he thought she was unduly influencing Brian. "Mostly we were just cold and hungry."

Pasco certainly looked concerned, she admitted. A dark stubble covered his jaw, and he seemed to have aged in the past day or two. His red eyes indicated he might have had a sleepless night himself. Well, he would be concerned, she thought, if he had hit them over the head, abandoned them on the ice, and then heard that they were alive and well. Very concerned.

Brian might be thinking the same thing. He was looking at Pasco a little warily.

"I figured you'd be out of town by now," he said to Pasco. "Kotzebue must have more attractions than I thought. Where's Wilson?"

"Haven't seen him all day. He said he had something to take care of, and he'd be in touch. He might have gone back to Anchorage. But—well, I couldn't leave until I knew you were okay."

The man actually sounded sincere, Malinche thought; worried, but sincere.

"Sit down," Brian said, perching on the foot of the bed, his face grim with purpose. "Joe, I have some questions, and I want you to be straight with me. We've been friends, and I don't forget that. But I need to know if you're involved in this—whatever it is.''

Pasco seemed to develop a strong interest in his fingernails. ''Brian, I'd tell you anything I know. But I don't know anything. You're right about one thing— there's pressure coming from somewhere. The best I can do is tell you to drop this thing.'' He glanced at Malinche. ''Whatever is going on, you two have a tiger by the tail.''

''Then if Universal Oil is involved, it's at a high level,'' Brian mused. ''But why are you following me around? It's too much to believe it's just coincidence.''

Joe shook his head miserably. ''I don't have a clue about what's going on. I was just told—to keep you in sight.''

''Who told you that?''

Pasco didn't respond. Brian would have pressed the issue, but the door, which Brian had neglected to lock after Joe's arrival, opened silently, and Jim Wilson entered the room.

''Hi,'' he said easily, his pale eyes making a quick survey. ''I wondered where everybody was. Anyone interested in dinner?''

Three pairs of eyes gazed at him in surprise. His mundane question did little to alleviate the tension in the room. If he felt it, he ignored it.

Joe spoke first. ''Well, hi, Jim. I thought you were long gone. You mentioned taking a plane out of here.''

''I'm leaving on the next flight,'' Wilson said, walking to the window and pulling aside the curtain. It was a casual movement, but Malinche knew the window afforded a good view of the street and the entrance to the hotel. ''I expect all of you will be doing the same.''

"Can't be too soon for me," Joe grumbled. "I wandered around all day, looking for something to do. Don't know what you found so fascinating."

"Lots of shops," Wilson said. "Good Native clothing."

"Yeah, I was in every one of them. Funny I didn't see you."

"I guess we missed each other." Wilson let the curtain fall and pulled out a straight backed chair. He sat there apparently quite at ease, relaxed, smiling. Nothing in his appearance accounted for Malinche's almost certain knowledge that he could spring to life in an instant, a snake striking. This wasn't a man who frequented local shops and looked at Native clothing.

He rose, stretched and glanced at Joe. "I'll be going down to the restaurant. You can all join me if you like. And Joe, I hope you'll join me on the flight back. I hate to fly alone. And maybe you two had better come along, too."

He left silence behind him. His invitation to Joe had sounded like an order. And his casual invitation to them had the ring of authority. For all his self-effacing manner, he acted as though he expected to be obeyed.

But it wouldn't work with her. Pasco might have to jump, even Brian, but Wilson had no authority over her. She could do as she pleased. Although the thought of being alone, without Brian, was scarier than she could admit even to herself.

Joe rose, again all smiles and expansiveness. "You two better come on down and have something to eat. And—maybe he's right. You should leave when we do."

"Is that an order, Joe?" Brian's voice was dangerously low.

Pasco hesitated. "Think about it," he finally said, and turned to follow Wilson out the door.

"So," Brian said, shutting the door and locking it. "What do you make of that? Wilson was nowhere to be seen for hours—and he could fit the description of one of the strangers Ganook said was hanging around the village."

"Do you think he was the one who attacked us?" Malinche whispered.

"He certainly could have been. He had the opportunity. But that still leaves that other guy, the one who could have been Carl Bettnor. Or maybe it was neither of them." He shook his head. "I don't see that we're a bit closer to finding out what happened to Dimitri. And we're not likely to, now that we don't even have the envelope."

"We don't need the envelope," Malinche said. "We have the return address. When we get back to Anchorage, we can try to find out why Dimitri was corresponding with the army."

"You're willing to go back to Anchorage now?"

"I don't see that we can do anything more here. We've traced Dimitri's last few days, and got a man killed in the process. And if Wilson is involved, he's going back to Anchorage. We may as well, too."

On the face of it, there was no reason her heart should feel so heavy. Dimitri's trail was cold; they had found out all they could here. But she wouldn't leave her brother's death unavenged; someone would pay. She could continue the investigation in Anchorage.

Her spurt of courage, when she had resolved to insist that Brian tell her his feelings, had vanished. He appeared as approachable and receptive as a granite rock. If he said nothing it was probably because he felt nothing, and she wasn't a woman who was interested in a one-way relationship. She knew it was in her nature to love wholeheartedly, give herself entirely, and she would never be happy with a man who couldn't reciprocate. Or if he did, managed to hide his feelings.

Yet, if she was honest with herself, she knew why she was depressed. Here, in Barrow and in the cave, even on the ice, she had lived life with an intensity she had never known existed. She had known, for a few idyllic hours, love. Love that existed only here when she was living on the edge. When she returned to her normal world, it would vanish. And unless Brian felt as she did, it would never be recovered.

Again she fingered the spot where the gold chain had lain; the lost talisman seemed a symbol of everything else she was losing.

"I still wonder why he took this dragon," she murmured. "He could have picked up one in any shop."

"Yeah. You're more familiar with Dimitri's work than I am. Can you think of anything at all that was different?"

"No." Slowly, painstakingly, she recreated the dragon in her mind. The same workmanship, the same size, the same dragon details. Yet something nagged at her, hovered around the edge of her mind. Had she looked carefully enough? Had she missed something?

Chapter Twelve

Malinche waited for Brian in her room. He had convinced her that they should follow Pasco and Wilson to the airport to be sure they actually got on the plane. She'd been reluctant to leave Kotzebue. With everything that had happened since leaving Anchorage, she still felt this interlude had been the most wonderful of her life.

And now they must leave; she didn't know what her relationship to Brian would be, but it would be different.

At his light tap, she opened the door. He stood there, lean and bronzed, gazing at her as though she were a vision that might vanish before his eyes. Was he, too, reluctant to leave this idyllic time behind?

Suddenly, as though unable to control himself, he moved toward her and clasped her in his arms. She came to him in a glad rush. His mouth sought hers, eager and demanding, sending bolts of lightning down every nerve. Warm and sensuous, his mouth captured hers, and she returned his kiss with a passion that shook her to her toes. She clung to him, in the grip of a desire so strong she could hardly stand.

Kicking shut the door, he moved her toward the bed.

"Malinche, Malinche..." He murmured her name like a benediction.

She moaned softly. His lips burned against her throat, the skin of her shoulder. Then she felt him move aside her shirt and bare her quivering breast to his seeking mouth. "I want you so much," he whispered. "Do you want me, Malinche? Say you do. I can't go back to Anchorage without—without—"

Her quick moves to assist in removing their clothing must have given her answer. They sank together onto the bed, entwined in the ancient movements of love. Nothing existed but the two of them, a man and a woman, in thrall to the elemental life force. All hesitancies, all thoughts, all problems, were swept aside as they crested the summit together.

Later, when their hearts had slowed a bit, he nuzzled her neck. "Heaven couldn't be any better than this."

She murmured assent—but was it heaven, or Eden which she feared they were about to leave? Surely now was the time to say he loved her—if he did. Or was this his way of saying goodbye?

STILL LATER, Brian came up to where she waited in the airport lounge. They'd had to wait most of the day for Wilson and Pasco to leave, and it was time to get their own flight underway. His impulse was to pull her to him, shower her with kisses, beg her to stay with him always, but he merely smiled. She pulled at his heart in so many ways—when she smiled, when she frowned, when she laughed—had he ever seen her cry? Yes, when she spoke of her brother, and her pain had torn at his heart. Her down jacket was zipped around her neck, but the hood lay along her back, baring her head which rose like a fragile flower from the fur trim.

He knew now the fragility was deceptive. Arctic flowers appeared delicate and fragile, but they withstood the harsh environment. She was like them—strong, tenacious, enduring.

Perhaps he had been wrong about her. Maybe she could stay the course. Whatever, he loved her and as soon as they got to Anchorage he would tell her so. He reached for her hand.

"Wilson and Pasco are on their way. I've serviced my plane. Come along, and we'll get Pete to check us out."

In the tower, Pete, a lanky man with a sharp face and dark blond hair caught back from his face in a ponytail, nodded and motioned them to a seat.

"Got a little disturbance coming up, Brian. Can you wait a sec while I check it out?"

"Sure."

A few minutes later Pete switched off the radio, shaking his head. "There's a bad storm out there, coming up fast."

"How bad is it?"

"Hard to say. You might stay ahead of it, but a small plane could be in trouble. And it will slow you down, for sure. Unless you're in a real hurry, I suggest you wait."

Smiling, Brian turned to Malinche. "How would you like to spend another day or so in beautiful downtown Kotzebue?"

THEY TOSSED THEIR BAGS down in front of the hotel counter, signed the register, and received keys for their room from a bored clerk. Malinche had no intention of staying alone even if Wilson and Pasco were far away. She'd had a midnight intruder before; it might have been Bettnor—or anyone—and they still might be near. Besides, after what had happened earlier between her and Brian, she didn't want to be more than a heartbeat away from him.

"Wait." Malinche glanced toward the lobby and paused, hand on the balustrade of the stairs. "Isn't that Ganook?"

Brian's gaze followed hers. Huddled in the armchair that he had drawn up close to the fireplace, the wizened little man appeared even smaller than he had in Netta's cabin. He appeared to be dozing, but at Malinche's words, his black eyes snapped open, alert as those of a bird of prey.

Leaving her luggage at the foot of the stairs, Malinche started toward him. "I wonder what he's doing here?" she whispered to Brian. Seen out of his element, among the trappings of civilization, he seemed even more archaic than when they had first seen him in the Eskimo village.

"Hello." She grasped the frail hand he held out to her in a firm handshake.

"We didn't expect to see you, Ganook. What are you doing here?"

"Waiting for you."

His matter-of-fact tone made her blink. "But—we had checked out. We should have been on our way to Anchorage. How did you know we'd be back?"

"Birds can't fly in weather like that." The old man gestured toward a narrow window. The wind, brisk when they left the airport, now roared around the building, sending shudders through its frame structure and rattling its glass.

"But the storm just started." It must have taken him an hour at least to get here from the village. "Even radar didn't pick up the disturbance until a few minutes ago.''

He shrugged, giving her an impatient look. ''White man's magic isn't the only way to find out what's going on.''

She felt firmly put in her place. Of course Eskimos hadn't survived in this harsh climate without becoming experts on predicting weather. She sat cross-legged on the floor beside him. A glance out of the corner of her eye showed Brian leaning one elbow on the driftwood mantel above the fireplace.

The two men presented such a contrast. The one, young, virile, pragmatic, strong; the other, old and shriveled, but with an air of knowledge and mysticism that was powerful in its own way. Here, side by side, they seemed to symbolize the two sides of her nature, pulling against each other.

''You've made a long trip for your age,'' she said gently, patting the old man's hand. ''Why are you here?''

''I have been thinking about what's been happening—the evil that has come to our people, the evil I still see hovering around you—and I thought I could be of more help.''

''You've thought of something else to tell us?''

Ganook gestured toward a high wingback chair. Its back had been turned to them, half obliterating its occupant, and Malinche had been so surprised to see Ganook that she hadn't noticed the other man. He had sat stiff and silent as a totem pole. Now he turned and regarded her with dark, opaque eyes. Mistrustful eyes, she decided.

''Come here, Ootek,'' Ganook commanded, his voice suddenly strong and clear.

Reluctantly, the other man stood and inched a couple of steps closer. His broad face and sturdy stature indicated he was an Eskimo, but although dressed in Native style, his clothing was somehow different from Ganook's. Each village, Malinche remembered, had its own minute difference in style.

"Ootek lives in a village just down the coast," Ganook said. "He came to Kotzebue for the Gathering. He had already gone home, and I asked him to return."

Ootek grunted and gave the older man a dark look. Asked? Malinche wondered, observing Ootek's surly manner. Ordered was more likely.

Ganook nodded sternly at Ootek. "Tell them."

Ootek gazed stubbornly at the floor. Ganook's voice became gentler. "It's all right. You're safe. These two seek the man who killed your friend. I know you were afraid to speak before, but this man and woman will help."

Ootek didn't look convinced, but he could not withstand the power of the shaman. In a low monotone, Ootek spoke, as though reciting words he had used over and over in his head. "I was at the Gathering. I became friends with Dimitri. I believe I was the last person to see him alive—except his killer, of course."

Brian gave a low whistle. "Then you're absolutely sure someone at the Gathering killed him?"

"Of course. They say he lost his way and froze to death. Ridiculous. He knew the ways of the North as well as I do. He hadn't planned to leave the Gathering. He was very excited. He said he was very close to finding a man for whom he'd been searching for a long time. A dangerous man. A man who had done him great harm. And when I last saw him, I saw the shadow of a man right behind him."

"Who was behind him? And who was he looking for?"

"I didn't see enough of the man to recognize him. As for whom he searched—he wasn't completely sure, although he had a good idea. He was searching for proof, I think. He said this man was evil—he deserved to die."

"Did you see any strangers around, get even a hint of who might have killed him?" Brian said.

Ootek shrugged. "There are always strangers at the Gathering. Reporters. Tourists. Government men trying to find out what we're talking about. They seem to think we're dangerous, as though we cared about their warring countries. They're the same to us. We just want to visit with friends and relatives, keep up our old customs."

Brian described Carl Bettnor. "Was he one of the strangers?"

"Yes, I remember him. A hard man, like old leather. He seemed very close to Dimitri. He was always talking to him."

"So, when did you last see Dimitri?"

"He was walking to the sauna. He liked to go late in the evening when it was often uncrowded. I never saw him again, although I waited where we had agreed to meet. He never came. I heard that his body was found the next day. An accident, they said. I left for home right away, to escape the evil."

"We know he was murdered now, but what made you so sure then?"

"I felt it," Ootek said. "I felt the evil around him, growing stronger each day. He felt it, too, and I know he was afraid, but he had to keep on. He had to find out.'' He glanced at Ganook. ''I have nothing more to say.''

''You have done well, son.'' Ganook struggled up from the chair and placed his frail hand on Ootek's arm, then turned to Malinche. ''I don't know if any of this helps. Most of it you knew, perhaps not all. Ootek was afraid to talk to you. He thought he might be killed as well. I persuaded him he must tell you everything for the sake of Dimitri and Charlie. Be on guard, the air still smells of evil.'' He shrugged deeper into his parka. ''We will go now.''

''But the storm is still fierce.'' Malinche raised her voice slightly to be heard above the sounds of force and fury still assaulting the building. ''Why don't you stay until this passes over?''

Ootek and Ganook gave her an identical, amused glance, and walked toward the door. A minute later they were lost to sight in the storm.

''Will they be all right?'' she whispered to Brian.

''They wouldn't have left if they didn't know what they were doing,'' he said. ''A storm that would stop a plane in the air might not stop ground travel. Let's go up to the room. We need to think about what they told us. We know who saw him last, but I'm not sure how much good that will do us.''

In the room, she instinctively turned to him, placing her cheek against the hard muscles of his chest. His heartbeat was strong, even through the clothing, giving her a feeling of comfort—and something much more unsettling. He kissed her thoroughly, then sank into a chair and pulled her onto his lap.

''Back again,'' he said softly.

She knew he was remembering, as she was, the ecstasy they had felt in this room. "Maybe something wants us to stay," she murmured.

"The Universe trying to tell us something?" he teased. "You sound as weird as that old shaman. I didn't want to fly back in a storm, and from the sounds of it, I was right."

Startled by a raucous sound, she glanced out the window and shivered. The force of the wind had sent a dozen tin cans rattling down the street. "How long do you think this weather will last?"

"Hard to tell. Perhaps we should have asked Ganook. Shamans seem to be able to foretell the weather. What the heck," he said, giving her a sly glance, "maybe he even conjured it up."

She smiled wanly at his little joke. He was trying to lighten her somber mood. He didn't share that age-old belief in the mystical that she was fighting hard to overcome. And she shivered at the conviction in the old man's voice when he spoke of evil.

"Well," Brian said, placing a kiss on the back of her neck, "we're doubly sure now that Bettnor was involved. Someone met Dimitri at the sauna. But was it Bettnor, or someone else? Was Bettnor there to kill Dimitri, or to keep an eye on him, maybe even protect him if he actually was a spy? Maybe the contact actually killed Stanislof."

"You're assuming Dimitri was really a spy," she said.

"It's something we have to consider. Or maybe Bettnor just thought he was a spy—we don't know. And how does Jim Wilson, a man from Universal Oil, fit in? From the description we were given, he must have been there when Charlie was killed. Perhaps he was at the Gathering, too."

She sighed. "I don't know. I'm completely confused. I'm just glad Wilson and Pasco are on the plane to Anchorage. And I sure wish I knew where Bettnor was right now."

Brian's gut tightened at the note of fear in her voice. Dark shadows of exhaustion circled her eyes. He pulled her tighter, wishing his arms could banish the fear. Her cheekbones were more pronounced than they had been; she had lost weight during the grueling ordeal on the ice.

His heart twisted with a tenderness so fierce it was almost painful. He would do anything to keep her safe. She was tired and vulnerable, not yet recovered from her loss of sleep and days without food. And, he thought, with a pang of guilt, he had made love to her, further using up her reserves. It was just as well she had a night to rest before they went home.

He also wished he knew where Bettnor was. But nothing was going to happen to her tonight—even if he had to spend all of it sitting by the door with a gun. Although he'd rather spend the night in her arms. How long had he known he loved her? Should he tell her now, or wait until they returned to Anchorage when they were both back in their familiar milieu and it made more sense to make plans for the future? He'd wait, he decided. He wanted just the right time and place.

"Why don't you take a shower?" he said softly. "You'll feel better. Then we'll hunt up some food."

"Sounds like a great idea." She yawned and stumbled toward the bathroom.

Brian lay back against the pillow, hands clasped behind his head, and listened to the rush of the shower, imagining its warmth cascading down her slender body. Why didn't he just slip off his clothes and join her?

But they were still in danger, sitting ducks if Bettnor or anyone else returned. He couldn't let his guard down. And lovemaking with Malinche was, to say the least, distracting.

Wrapped in a skimpy hotel towel, she emerged from the shower drowsy and warm and scurried into bed. He needn't have wondered whether to approach her. She was asleep almost before her head hit the pillow.

"So much for food," he murmured, tucking the blanket up under her chin. For several moments he gazed down at her, his heart pounding, noticing the sweep of black lashes against her ivory cheek, the softness of her half-parted lips. How much could a man take?

Sighing, he took his revolver from his pack and positioned a chair to face the door. It was going to be a long night.

MALINCHE GLANCED covertly at Brian's face as he dropped altitude and skimmed over the bowl that held the city of Anchorage. After the barren landscape they had just left, the city appeared lush and welcoming. Friendly. Not at all like Brian, who seemed distracted by thoughts of his own.

He eased the plane down onto the surface of the small lake. It seemed a lifetime had elapsed since they had lifted into the sky on their adventure. She had been hopeful then. Now she had a hard time fighting off misery—and anger. Was Brian going to ignore everything that had happened between them?

They had awakened that morning to a clear sky and gone immediately to the airport. Brian appeared tired, but her long sleep had rejuvenated her. She had hoped they might make love, but wasn't assertive enough to suggest it. As for Brian, his mind seemed on something else.

She was right back where she started, she thought, both figuratively and literally. What had she gained by this trip? She had learned more about Dimitri, enough to sharpen the constant pain that came because she had never known her own brother. But she was just as far from finding out who had killed him. Even the dragon talisman was gone, and if it had harbored an elusive clue, it was lost, too. Yet something about it—about the carving of the head—nagged at her.

And how could she have thought an envelope, with only a return address, could tell her anything helpful? In retrospect, it seemed ridiculous to think she could trace it and find out what its contents had been. And an innocent man was dead, just because he had tried to help them.

As for Brian, she was no closer to discovering his true feelings, either. She had more pride than to force herself on a man who wanted no commitment.

He was an attractive man. A sexy man. A man who'd shown her passion she'd never believed possible. An admirable, courageous man. Perhaps she believed she loved him because they had faced so much danger together. He was her protector, her chance for survival.

Now she could think more clearly. This virile, wonderful man had a flaw. He was too wary to ever give his heart to any woman. And she wasn't a masochist. She knew she could love—he had taught her how much she had to give—but he had also taught her he could never reciprocate.

What should she do now? The trail to her brother's killer had run out. Whoever had been chasing them must know that, too, and he wouldn't pursue. She suspected that now they were in Anchorage she would see little of Brian.

But her reason for coming to Alaska still remained. The last few days had confirmed her need to find her own identity, but she was less sure of herself than she had ever been. She had felt a strong affinity for Netta, Ganook, for their way of life, but she knew it could never be hers. Yet life with her father in his rarefied world of power and high finance seemed just as remote. Where was her place?

The plane taxied up to the pier and Malinche jumped out to secure the rope to the piling. As Brian tossed the bags down, she glanced a little fearfully toward the shore. They hadn't notified anyone when they left Kotzebue, but it would be a simple matter for someone to check their takeoff time.

Pasco or Wilson or both might be waiting for them. Keeping track of them.

But no familiar figures stood at the beginning of the pier. She didn't see a thing except a huge black limousine parked in the lot....

Her pulse skipped a beat. She stood transfixed, as the vehicle door opened and a tall, bulky man stepped out onto the tarmac.

She raced toward the distant figure, arms outstretched.

"Daddy!"

Buck Adams enfolded his daughter in his powerful arms.

Chapter Thirteen

Brian secured the rope to the piling, and followed Malinche up the pier. He didn't hurry. Malinche's glad cry of "Daddy!" made him certain that the man who held her in a warm hug was the legendary Buck Adams. He would have guessed it anyway. Even at his advanced age, everything about the man—his confident bearing, his clothing—cried power and money, both things which Brian regarded warily.

As he traversed the short distance, Brian took his time in assessing the man. He'd read about him and seen photos, but they didn't convey the sense of raw power that seeing Adams in person did. Buck Adams was big—big all over. The suit, obviously tailor-made, was of the finest silk. His coarse black hair showed wide streaks of gray. Thick-jawed, barrel-chested, thighs like trees, he had planted himself on the deck, and his manner said only a foolhardy man would try to displace him.

Buck shifted his attention from Malinche to look Brian directly in the eyes. The man was elderly, but he was formidable in every respect, not just in appearance. Deep, penetrating, intelligent, his eyes gazed out of a wrinkled face, seeming to see everything at once.

Brian remembered what he had heard of the man: Buck Adams had knocked about all over the world before, having made and lost a couple of fortunes, he had struck gold in Alaska. That was only the start of the fortune he had amassed. Smart, energetic, ruthless, he had parlayed that strike into one of America's biggest financial empires.

And this was Malinche's father, the man she could turn to anytime she wished. It was a sobering thought.

Malinche turned from her father's embrace. "Dad, this is Brian Kennedy. He's—he's been a big help to me."

Buck smiled, a smile that had sparked terror in many a man, and grasped Brian's hand. Brian gripped it firmly, Buck's grip grew firmer, Brian squeezed tighter—and then relaxed. He couldn't believe he was involved in the old masculine ritual of dominance.

Besides, he couldn't blame Buck for his wariness. Not only was his daughter beautiful, she was excessively rich, and that would be an unbeatable combination for many men. For Brian, it didn't work that way. He wanted his wife to live in his world, and why would anyone give up the world Buck could provide for what he could offer? He had decided that when they reached Anchorage he would tell Malinche he loved her, see if they could work out a future. That seemed naive now. He had only to remember the joy in her voice when she called out to her father to realize how hopeless his dream was.

"Glad to meet you," Buck said. "I hear you and my little darling have been having quite an adventure."

Little Darling! "Where did you hear that?" Obviously Buck, although unseen, had been keeping close track of his daughter.

"We'll talk later," Buck said, glancing at Malinche. "Let's get back to the apartment, little girl, and talk about what you've been up to." The harshness vanished from his eyes, replaced by tenderness. He had one vulnerable spot, Brian saw.

A man unaccustomed to arguments about his decisions, he was already leading the way to the limousine.

Malinche, clutching his hand, laughed up into her father's face. She had nothing to fear now, Brian thought sourly, now that "Daddy" was here to fix everything.

"A limousine, Dad?" she teased. "And a suit? Don't you know you're out of style up here?"

"Style?" he growled. "I didn't give it much thought. When I got the word, I came up in a hurry."

"What word? And how did you know where and when we were going to land?"

Buck shook his head impatiently. "I didn't know exactly when you'd be here—I've been waiting for hours. As to where you'd land—I was told where Kennedy here kept his plane. Now, let's get back to your apartment so you can rest up a bit."

"Dad, I've done nothing but rest for the past few hours."

"A little more won't hurt you." He nodded curtly to Brian. "You, too." He ushered Malinche into the back seat and climbed in beside her.

Brian bristled at the man's tone, but he decided to ignore it. Adams was used to commanding; he probably didn't give his brusque manner a thought, and there was no reason to make an issue of it. That didn't mean he would meekly obey.

"Sorry. I've got my Jeep parked here. I'll drive it."

"I'll send someone for it. Get in."

Brian shrugged. Other than fight over a minor matter, there seemed nothing else to do. Besides, he wanted to be near Malinche; there were matters that must be decided between them. Although Buck's presence put things in a different light. He had been nearly sure she loved him, but with Buck here, he wondered if he should wait awhile before he said anything....

The limo swung out onto the highway and headed toward Anchorage. Brian paid little attention to the conversation between Malinche and her father. It was mainly gossip about famous and wealthy people that Brian didn't know—and didn't want to know.

As they swung into Muldoon Street, Brian turned to them. "I have to go my place first. You can drop me off."

"Drop you off? You're coming with us, Kennedy."

Brian's jaw set, and he glanced at the formidable Buck Adams. The other man's eyes drilled into his.

"I don't take orders, Mr. Adams," Brian said quietly. He'd had as much of this treatment as he planned on taking. "I don't work for you."

Buck appeared genuinely surprised. Then he grinned. "No, you don't work for me, do you? As a father, though, I want to talk to you. Will you *please* come along with us?"

Brian nodded, feeling rather ridiculous. This was nothing to make an issue of. He was reacting as he usually did to authority—rebelliously. Malinche had rebelled against Buck's authority, too. But how much had she really rebelled, and how soon would she revert to being "Daddy's Little Darling"?

A few moments later Malinche flung open the door to her apartment and scrutinized it closely before stepping inside. Everything looked just as she had left it:

the elegant sofa positioned on the plush carpet, the richly upholstered chair across from it, the highly polished coffee table with a magazine still open on it. If anyone had been there while she was gone they had left no sign.

Brian followed closely with her luggage. "Where do you want these?"

"Just put them on the floor," Buck said, gravitating to the most comfortable chair in the room. It appeared fragile under his weight. "Sit down. We've got things to talk about."

Malinche glanced at Brian's mutinous expression, and smiled inwardly as he sat on the couch beside her. She'd had years to become used to Buck's autocratic manner, and it still rankled her sometimes. Certainly it was annoying Brian. In some ways the two were alike—stubborn, determined—and dependable. She suspected she had been upset by Brian's manner at first because it was so much like Buck's which she was trying to evade. Now that Buck was here her earlier rebellion seemed childish.

Buck glared at them for a few seconds. "Now, you two, just what in hell has been going on around here? I was called by a real concerned guy—he said I better get up here fast."

"Who?" Malinche demanded. "Who called you?"

"Never mind who. I gathered you two were stirring up a hornet's nest and everybody would be a lot better off if you came on home with me, girl. So—talk."

Malinche and Brian exchanged glances. Brian wasn't saying anything. It was up to Malinche.

For the next hour, Buck sat still, interrupting only to clear up a point, while Malinche told him what had happened from the time Dimitri had called her on the phone and left his message. When she had finished, Buck gave a huge sigh. If she hadn't known better, Malinche might have thought his eyes misted with tears. He seemed lost in memories. Pain flashed in his eyes.

"Dimitri, my son. I always thought he was dead. If I had known..."

The fleeting expression was gone. He hadn't known, and Buck was a pragmatist. He wouldn't cry over something he couldn't change. Shrugging off whatever he felt, he turned to Malinche. "Well, I see they didn't exaggerate. Pack your things, girl. My jet is at the airport. We'll get out of here right now."

"No."

"No?" He leaned forward and pounded his hammy fist on his silk-clad knee. "Don't talk to your dad like that. Good God, don't you realize the danger you're in? It was a silly idea, your coming up here to 'find your roots.' And now you're mixed up in something truly dangerous. I don't know where your roots are, but your life is with me, where I can protect you—"

"Dad, Dimitri was your son! My brother! You must have loved him. He deserves—"

"He's dead, and nothing will change that. And you're alive, although you were almost killed. Pack your things."

"I'm not going back with you, Dad. I can't quit while I'm in the middle of something—"

"You haven't the slightest idea what you're in the middle of. And neither do I."

"I don't mean just finding out who murdered Dimitri. Maybe I can't do that, as much as I try, but I can't quit. Don't you see? I have to be on my own for a while, find out who I am without you paving the way for me.''

"The old 'lost identity' thing! I didn't buy it before, and I don't now. You're my daughter—''

"I'm my mother's daughter, too.''

"Yes." His eyes softened. "I see that more and more. She was old to have a baby when she had you, but she insisted. She rarely listened to reason, either. If she had lived—'' He shrugged away the memory and returned to the attack.

Brian listened silently, hoping Malinche would not give in. It would be best for everyone if she did; her stubbornness now would only postpone her eventual compliance. And Buck wouldn't give up the war just because he might lose a battle or two. It was merely a matter of time.

"All right,'' Buck finally said, "so, you're not coming home. But I can't leave you here with things unresolved and somebody out to kill you. Can I do anything to help?''

It was possible he could. Brian thought of the blank walls they encountered every time they approached the authorities. Buck had power and influence. He elected senators, made and destroyed companies and careers, was a mover and shaker. Perhaps he could do what Brian and Malinche couldn't—get some answers.

"If we could find out what was in that letter from the army, we might not be at a complete dead end. Why was the Department of the Army interested in Dimitri?'' Brian said. "Can you find out?''

Buck thought a minute. "I could make a call or two,'' he finally said.

"The phone is—''

"Not from here. The phone is probably bugged.

Since it seems I'll be here awhile, I'll check into a hotel and call from there. I'll be back.''

Brian listened to the limo pull away, and cursed himself for not thinking of the possibility of phones being bugged. Malinche had also looked surprised. Now she slid back in her chair and closed her eyes. Brian understood her reaction. When Buck left, he seemed to suck the energy from the room. Brian wanted to go to her, smooth the frown from her face, tell her he loved her and would take care of her. It seemed ridiculous. Buck had changed everything. Not the love, of course, but Brian's hope that it would work out between them. She didn't need him to protect her—she had Buck.

''Who do you think put a burr under his collar and sent him rushing up to rescue you?'' he asked.

She smiled wanly. ''That's hard to say. Dad has his fingers in a lot of pies. He has a spy system to rival the CIA.''

''You stood up to him.'' What would happen if he went over and took her in his arms? Could he possibly be part of the reason she had insisted on staying? She was one hell of a woman, stronger than he ever would have suspected. But not strong enough to resist to the end, he thought, staying where he was.

He mustn't give in to his dreams. She had stood up to Buck this time, but she said herself she had an inner conflict as to where she belonged. In the end her background would win out, and she would return to her life of privilege. Any woman would. And what could he offer her beside what Buck offered?

He paced the floor until Buck returned, trying to control his emotions, aware that she watched him from under partly closed eyelids.

''Well,'' the man said, plopping down in the chair

and running a silk handkerchief across his forehead, "you two have gotten yourselves into more trouble than I expected."

Adams seemed to have aged in the hour since he had left the apartment. His shoulders sagged, and the lines in his flushed face showed every one of his years. His glance at Malinche showed definite concern.

"What did you find out?" Brian asked.

"Something that makes me more worried than ever. I talked to a friend of mine in the Pentagon. He owes me some favors...he dug around. Said Dimitri Stanislof had requested the names of any soldiers who had served at Ward Cove during the War."

"So, did he say what the answer was?"

Buck shook his head. "No, that's what's so disturbing. He didn't know who answered the letter—it had been sent up the line someplace. He said he'd check and call back. He did call back—and suddenly he didn't know anything about anything. He thought he might even have been mistaken about the original request. This from a friend of mine! I saved his life once, I'd trust him with mine."

"But didn't you get a hint—a clue?"

"The hint, if you call it that, is that this affair goes high up. He didn't say so, but I suspect either CIA involvement or pressure from an oil cartel. Nothing else would scare him so much that he'd forget our friendship."

"Why would you suspect an oil cartel?"

Buck rubbed his hand over his eyes. "The man who told me to get up here fast because my daughter was in danger was an oil man."

Damn. Brian had hoped there would be no more ties to Universal Oil, but the coincidences were too many to ignore. He felt as though he had lived his entire life in innocence. Pasco must be in this up to his ears.

"Dimitri must have had more influence than I thought," he said. "He was dead set against drilling on ANWR—the Arctic National Wildlife Refuge—and I know they thought he was a nuisance. But murder? And could an oil company silence the police? That sounds more like the government to me."

Buck rose slowly to his feet, suddenly showing every one of his advanced years, an old man as he gazed at his beloved daughter. "I don't know. If I could, I'd pick you up and carry you out of here, Malinche. I guess I wouldn't leave myself if someone was trying to chase me away. But you know how dangerous it is."

"I'd say we've had proof of that," Brian said wryly.

"You've been lucky," Buck retorted. "It may not keep up." He stood and enfolded Malinche in his arms. "If you're positive you won't come back, I may as well leave. Call if you change your mind—or need anything at all. Take care, darlin'."

Recovering his autocratic manner, he turned to Brian. "Step outside, Kennedy. I'd like a word with you in private."

"Dad—"

"In private, I said."

Grinning at Malinche's outraged expression, Brian followed Buck out the door. He strode to the vehicle, not once glancing back. Only when the older man was seated in the back of the limo did he turn to Brian. "You love her, don't you, boy?"

"What! I—" This was the last thing Brian had expected.

Buck waved his hand, cutting him off. "Don't

bother to deny it. I can see it in your face, every time you look at her. Every time she looks at you, for that matter. So, I have a proposition for you.''

Brian gazed back in amazement. Yes, of course he loved her, had from the minute he saw her. But he suspected Buck wouldn't understand that love wasn't enough when two lives were as separate as his and Malinche's. Besides, it was really none of the old man's business.

"I also think I know why you're holding back," Buck said. "You don't strike me as a man who would ordinarily do that. You'd go after what you wanted. But you're hesitating because she's rich and you're poor.''

Brian's jaw tightened. If it were only that simple. Besides, he didn't consider himself poor, although maybe to people like Buck he was.

Buck apparently didn't need confirmation of his assessment. "Here's my proposition. I've got plenty of jobs for a man like you—or you can make your own. Name your own terms. Just bring my little girl home. Does that sound so bad? Money and the girl you love?''

Brian struggled between laughing and exploding in anger. Neither, on reflection, seemed appropriate. The man loved his daughter, and was trying to protect her. If that included buying a son-in-law, that was cheap. He couldn't be expected to know Brian couldn't be bought.

"I'm afraid I wouldn't have any more success in getting her home than you've had, sir. She seems to be her own woman.''

"Nuts. She's crazy about you. If I didn't know that, and how you feel about her, I'd never leave her here.

She's all I've got, Kennedy, and I'm trusting you to protect her.''

"I'd planned on doing that," Brian ground out.

"I wouldn't leave her with just any man, but I'm a good judge of character. You watch out for her—or you'll answer to me."

"You don't need to threaten me. Of course I'll watch out for her."

"If anything happens to her—"

"It won't."

"Okay, I know you'll do your best. It had damn well better be enough." He held Brian's eyes for a long moment. Then signaled his driver to go.

Brian stared after the limo. He felt as though he'd been in the presence of a force of nature. Not too often does a man get offered the position of son-in-law with a cushy life, and threatened in the same breath. He had to admit he was flattered by Buck's assessment of him. Trusting him to protect his only daughter. Brian knew he would—with his life, if necessary.

But hadn't Buck given up too easily?

Maybe Buck believed that with the theft of the dragon, they were no longer in danger. Brian didn't.

She was waiting at the door, arms crossed over her chest, looking angry enough to chew nails. "So, did the menfolk get my future all taken care of?"

"Hey, what makes you think we were talking about you?"

"Let me tell you exactly what he said. If you'll convince me to go home, he'll give you a fabulous reward!"

"If he believed that I could influence you, he doesn't know you as well as I do. Convincing you to do something for your own good is like getting water to run uphill. It's not a bad idea, though. We've run out of options."

"There seems to be a connection to Ward Cove," she said slowly, dropping her arms to her side.

"How do you figure that?"

"All the strings connect. My mother was in Ward Cove, although she was only a child when the War ended and she left. I wonder if she knew Dimitri? And why was Dimitri interested in the name of a soldier who had served there?"

"I don't see how your mother figures in this at all. And you said Dimitri was a child of four or five when he left there."

"I know. I wish so much he'd lived." Her voice trailed away, then with an obvious effort, she continued. "He could have told me so much about what life was like for her there—I think if I'd known that, what shaped her, little stories about her, I would feel so much closer to her."

He hated to see the pain in her eyes. "We'd better think of something to eat," he said, more to divert her than because he was hungry. "Check the freezer, and I'll dash over to my place for messages."

"I'll come with you. We can stop off at a grocery store."

In Brian's apartment, Malinche lingered by the door while Brian checked the messages on his machine. Joe Pasco's voice came clearly through the machine.

"Brian? Aren't you home yet? Well, give me a call the minute you get in. I need to see you. It's urgent."

Brian shut off the machine and riffled through a pile of letters.

"Are you going to call him?"

"No." Brian replaced the stack of mail that his landlady had left on his desk. "I think we need a break, without anybody looking over our shoulder. I see your efficient father had my Jeep delivered here. Let's get the groceries and have a huge steak, a glass of wine, and a nice quiet evening."

After the strain of the past few days, it sounded heavenly. They wandered through the grocery store, Brian pushing the basket while Malinche dropped in items: two sirloin steaks, a head of lettuce, a cucumber, mushrooms, onions, two baking potatoes. Brian was a steak-and-potatoes man.

Such a comforting, domestic feeling engulfed her that the events of the past few days seemed to have happened to someone else. Tonight, she was determined to push all problems and fears aside and have a quiet evening with Brian. Or maybe it wouldn't be so quiet, after all. Maybe he would drop his emotional barrier, or maybe she would be assertive and demand they talk about their relationship. The night stretched ahead with endless possibilities.

Later, she popped the potatoes in the microwave and made the salad while Brian broiled the steaks. He seemed as content as she, although he did seem preoccupied. Was he still thinking about his discussion with her father? She knew Buck so well she was certain she knew what he'd said to Brian—he'd offered him a job if he returned her to Seattle. How would she feel, living in the lower forty-eight with Brian? It had lovely possibilities. Maybe she should forget her obsession with Dimitri and get on with her life.

After dinner, they sat together on the sofa, his arm around her waist. Malinche let her head rest lightly on his shoulder. If she gave up the pursuit of Dimitri's killer, what would happen between her and Brian? Her conflict was still here, eating a hole in her heart. She was no closer to coming to terms with her past than when she had first arrived in Alaska.

She moved a hairbreadth away; instinctively, his arm tightened around her. Slowly, gently, he leaned over and kissed her, a gentle kiss that rapidly turned passionate, sending currents of heat all through her body. When he pulled away, he said huskily, "We need to talk."

Her heart raced. She hadn't needed to force the issue. "Yes, we do."

"I think I'd better stay here tonight."

Something had changed. His voice held a hint of uneasiness. Disappointment lodged in her throat. That didn't sound like the beginning of a declaration of love.

"Still on guard duty?"

"Maybe. Did you notice anything strange while we were driving to my apartment tonight, and then to the grocery store?"

"No." A chill ran down her spine. Suddenly the outside world had intruded on their intimate evening.

"I didn't want to alarm you until I was sure. I'd hoped they'd given up. But I'm positive someone is following us."

"But I didn't see anyone."

"He's a pro. He's driving a gray sedan. I kept catching glimpses of him, and then I'd lose him. He knew enough to stay well back."

The fear, the sense of evil dogging their footsteps, rushed back all the more strongly for having been displaced for a few hours. Her familiar apartment was vulnerable. Shivering, she crowded closer to the warmth and comfort of Brian's lean body. "Are—are you sure?"

"He's parked about a block up the street right now."

Chapter Fourteen

Malinche rushed to the window and pushed aside the drapes. About halfway up the next block a dusty gray sedan was parked neatly against the curb. Her heart plunged, all the terror of the past few days flooding back.

Someone was keeping track of their every move. Buck's surprise visit had made her feel more secure than she actually was.

Brian came up behind her and gazed over her shoulder. She inched a little closer. The need to be near him wasn't caused entirely by fear. Somehow she felt more—more herself—when their bodies touched.

"Do you recognize him?"

By the breadth of his shoulders, she could see that a man sat behind the wheel, but she was unable to make out his features. "No—he's too far away."

"We'll fix that." Brian moved with the swiftness of a panther. He was out the door before Malinche could protest. Was he planning to confront the man? He had no idea of who he was or whether he was armed. It was the height of insanity, but there was nothing she could do to stop him. He was already out of sight among the bushes that fringed the backyard.

She kept her eyes on the gray sedan, afraid its occupant would spot them. Thankfully, he seemed to suspect nothing. He shifted restlessly and laid his head back against the seat. If, as Brian said, he'd been following them for hours, he was probably bored and tired.

She stiffened as Brian appeared, bent low and running behind a board fence several yards behind the car. Holding her breath, she saw him step out onto the sidewalk. He was strolling, head down, apparently immersed in thought. She saw his strategy. The watcher was parked where he could see her apartment. He wouldn't expect anyone to come from a different direction. A casual passerby posed no threat.

Brian was even with the front door of the vehicle, still ambling along. Suddenly he turned with lightning-like speed and swung open the door. He grabbed the watcher by the back of his jacket and jerked him out onto the sidewalk.

On his knees on the grass, the man gazed wildly up. Brian stood above him, hands clenched. Even taken off guard, the man was formidable. He scrambled to his feet and aimed a punch that, had it connected, would have sent Brian sprawling. Luckily, it glanced off Brian's arm. Brian aimed a right at the man's jaw, hard enough to stagger him.

But not for long. The man rushed back swinging, landing blows that shoved Brian back against the car.

Paralyzed, Malinche watched the tableau. Should she call the police? Long ago, in another world, that would have been her first response. Now such an action seemed naive at best.

She bit her lip, feeling the blow herself, as the stranger slammed Brian up against the car; then she let out a long breath as Brian sent a shuddering blow to the man's jaw. As far as she could tell, the battle was nearly equal.

She couldn't just stand there hiding behind the drapes! Picking up a heavy brass candlestick from the foyer table, she raced out the door and up the walk.

By the time she reached them, the contest was over. Brian, breathing heavily, had the man pinned against the car and one arm twisted behind his back.

"Here comes the cavalry." One eye was swollen and there was blood on his lip, but he managed a jaunty grin.

"Are you all right?"

"Better off than he is. Let's get this guy in the apartment where we can talk to him."

"Let me go!" The man twisted futilely against Brian's grip.

"Let you go? Not until we get a few answers." Brian increased the pressure until the man winced with pain.

Held captive by Brian's firm grip on his arm, the man walked slowly toward the apartment. Malinche glanced around, hoping no one would come out asking questions, but they reached the door without interference.

Brian shoved the man inside. "Don't try anything. We're going to get some answers."

The man rubbed his arm and gave Brian an angry glare. At close range, he didn't look so intimidating. Probably in his early thirties, slim and fit, his close-cropped hair and erect posture gave the impression of military training, but his denims, flannel shirt and logger's boots belied it.

"Who are you? And why were you following us?"

Brian's stance was deceptively casual; he stood on the balls of his feet, his fists lightly curled.

The man stared mutely back, his lips tightly compressed.

"Come on, talk!"

Coolly insolent, the man did not reply.

Suddenly, like a spring released, Brian leaped across the room. He shoved the man roughly into a chair and glared down at him. "Listen to me. We're not playing around. You're not getting out of here until you talk, and it might get uncomfortable!"

The man's gaze wavered; he rubbed his arm, and fingered his jaw where the mark of Brian's fist remained. Then he shrugged, his decision made. "Okay. I didn't hire on to get beat up. He said it would be easy work. Just keep an eye on you and her and report in. If anything happened, I was to radio for help."

"Radio who? Who in the hell are you? And who hired you?"

"My name's Smith. Jerry Smith. As to who hired me—" he nodded toward Malinche "—the little lady's father."

"Dad! That can't be true," Malinche protested. "Why would he hire you to spy on us?"

"I was just supposed to follow you, see to it that you didn't get into trouble. He never said I'd have to fight a wildman." He gave Brian a resentful glance.

"I can't believe this. He actually hired you to keep track of me?"

"He said you were stubborn, and to keep out of sight. You'd be upset. Guess he was right."

"You sure wouldn't have been much help if someone *was* threatening her," Brian growled.

"You were lucky. Or, maybe I was careless. If I'd

have had a second longer, I'd have had a gun at your back.''

"So, now what?" Brian's grin wasn't at all friendly. "What are you going to tell 'Daddy' now? That you blew it?"

Smith scrutinized his boots carefully. "I figure I won't have to say anything. I haven't hurt you guys. I can just keep watch, like I was doing. And you can pretend you never saw me."

"Why should we? We should turn you over to the police."

"The old man didn't tell me much, but enough to make me doubt you'll do that."

Brian glanced at Malinche. "What do you think? Is he telling the truth?"

"Probably." She sighed. "I was surprised when Dad left without putting up more of a fight. Maybe we should just let him go. Another set of eyes won't hurt."

Smith vaulted out of the chair, reaching for the doorknob.

"Okay," Brian said. "But remember, if we caught on to you, someone else could, too. You'd better be more alert."

"You bet." The door slammed behind him.

Malinche swung between laughter and anger. Her fright had been for nothing, but she still felt the effects tingling along her skin. And Buck had a heck of a nerve. He had promised to let her live her own life. From the thunderous look on Brian's face, he wasn't happy with Buck, either.

"So, 'Daddy' to the rescue." Brian threw himself down into the chair Smith had just vacated. He knew Malinche didn't deserve his sarcasm; it wasn't her doing. But when he remembered the urgency with which

Buck had asked him to protect her, he blazed with anger. To think he had actually been flattered. The man had manipulated him; he hadn't trusted him at all.

Malinche flushed. Brian was being completely unreasonable—not unusual for him! Still, she replied evenly. "He's always been overly protective. It's a habit he can't seem to break."

"I wonder who else he has roaming around keeping track of you. I'd like to know before I beat up another innocent guy."

"Well, he doesn't believe in doing things halfway."

"Great. So, now we won't know whether the bad guys or your bodyguards are after us. It adds a bit of spice to the situation."

"You needn't be so sarcastic. Dad was just concerned about me. It's nothing to get your ego in an uproar over. Maybe he was right—"

"He was right about one thing! You should go on home. Where he can keep an eye on you."

"I certainly don't intend to do that, no matter what either of you say!"

Brian saw the determination on her face. She didn't know when to call it quits, a dangerous habit to have. But she was no longer his responsibility. With a father like Buck Adams who probably had bodyguards stationed behind every tree, she didn't need Brian. Not to protect her.

Not for anything else, either. His heart sank as his dreams slipped away. He'd been right about her all along. She might say she wanted to be her own person, but she was glad Buck was involved. The best he could do for her was to persuade her to go home.

"Don't be so darn stubborn. Look at the trouble you've got into so far, and the trouble you got everyone else into." That wasn't entirely fair. He'd gotten himself into this by finding Dimitri's body, but he wasn't going to say so.

"You promised—"

"You don't need me. If you won't go home, just call 'Daddy' if you get in more trouble. Who knows how many men he has looking out for you."

If he sounded bitter, he couldn't help it. What really rankled was the feeling Buck had made a fool of him, didn't value him at all. He had promised to take care of her, given his word, which he didn't give lightly. Buck had only pretended to trust him. He would always be hovering over Malinche, and she wouldn't complain. With the arrogance of power and money, he had taken the matter into his own hands, showed Brian he considered him worse than useless.

It hurt that it was fine with Malinche. She was accustomed to having her father smooth over the rough spots. If ever Brian hoped he might have a future with Malinche, this showed he had been a fool. She would never have to commit herself to anything. When things got rough, she need only lift the phone and Adams would come running to the rescue. She could play house until she got bored, then return to the life-style that was her heritage.

"Brian, don't be upset. I know he sometimes goes overboard, but he loves me. It has nothing to do with you."

Her soft voice was entirely too persuasive; it made him even angrier. "It has everything to do with me. I'm not in his league. You are. So, why don't you go on home where you belong and make everybody happy? Get out of my hair."

Stung nearly to tears, she lashed back. "And you

know where I belong? How marvelous—that's more than I know. For a while I thought we belonged together. Was our lovemaking just to pass the time? As for not being in Buck's league, if you can ignore what happened between us, if you can say you'd be happy if I left, maybe you're *not* in his league. Buck would never let anybody down.''

''I'm not letting you down. You'll be safe—you have plenty of backup.''

She took a long deep breath to steady herself. How could she have been so wrong about Brian? He actually sounded jealous of Buck, but not because of her. Because he felt he'd been dismissed.

''All right,'' she said slowly, her shoulders sagging in defeat. ''I know I started all this. You said from the beginning you didn't want to be involved—with Dimitri—or me. But there in the cave there were times when I thought—differently.''

''Look, Malinche, I don't want you to misunderstand. Making love with you was the most wonderful experience of my life. I'll always treasure it. But we both knew it was a fantasy world. Everything was colored, made more intense, by the danger we were in. We're back in the real world, now. And it isn't the same. We're as far apart as two people can be. Whatever you believe that you feel now, it'll change the minute you go back to the life Buck made for you. You couldn't handle the kind of life I lead.''

He wished her soft underlip wouldn't tremble so. He loved her more than anything, even his own life, and he was making her miserable. But it was better for both of them in the long run.

She drew herself up to her full height, and gave him a long level look. All her pride, all her anger was in that look. She was her father's daughter. "If that's the way you feel, you'd better go."

"I—"

"Now."

He opened his mouth to speak, thought better of it, and let himself out the door. There was a bottle of whisky in his kitchen cabinet. He wasn't a drinker, but tonight looked like a perfect time to begin. He would try anything to blot her out of his mind. And the way he had acted toward her. He knew why he'd picked a fight, of course. She was getting too close.

He glanced at the gray sedan. It was still parked along the curb. Apparently Smith, if that was his name, didn't fancy telling Buck Adams that he had been found out. He was still on the lookout. That was good. He could leave with a clear conscience. If someone threatened Malinche tonight, Smith would stop him. The man would be more careful and not be caught napping after what Brian had put him through.

Malinche didn't go to the window to watch Brian drive away. She wasn't sure her pride and resolve would stretch that far. Tears rolled slowly down her cheeks; she didn't brush them away, knowing they came as much from anger as sorrow—anger at herself that she had nearly pleaded with him to stay, sorrow that the glimpse of his broad shoulders, his long legs, his easy grace, was the last she would see of him. Ever. Thank God she had found her pride before she made an absolute fool of herself.

Knowing this was the way it had to be helped some. Deep down, she had always known she had no future with Brian, although she had allowed herself to hope. But face it—a man who can't bring himself to admit he loves you is no prize.

But it wrenched her soul to watch him walk out of her life. She knew she loved him. In spite of everything, she loved him. But love isn't enough, not when two people are as different as she and Brian.

What should she do now? She couldn't just sit here in this chair, letting waves of depression wash over her. She had to think, make a plan, come to a decision. But that could wait until tomorrow. She lowered her head into her hands and sobbed.

THE MAN IN the dark van halfway down the block hung his earphones on a hook, and smiled. It was a smug, self-satisfied smile that those who knew him had learned to dread. After a less than auspicious start, things were going just fine.

He'd taken great pains to be inconspicuous. This was the kind of neighborhood where a strange automobile might be noticed. He had located a house where the owners would be gone for a couple of weeks, and parked in the driveway, partially screened by trees.

The sounds of their voices had come through loud and strong, and why shouldn't they? He was an expert at bugging houses, and his equipment was state-of-the-art. He had wired both apartments while Malinche and Brian were out. It could detect a whisper a mile away. He smiled when he thought of old Adams going out of the house to make a call, suspecting that both apartments were wired. He guessed Adams had made his call from a hotel room, but it didn't really matter. He had heard as much as he needed to.

He'd learned all he needed to know, and he still shook when he realized how close he'd come to disaster. He'd had so many chances to kill her, and she had survived every one. She had more lives than a cat! Or maybe he was losing his touch after years of easy success. No one, not even the devil himself, should have been able to escape that ice floe.

It didn't matter, though, not in the long run. He had the dragon, and they never would have found out anything from the envelope. Even Buck Adams couldn't, with all his connections.

And now the boyfriend was stalking off in a huff. Not that he could trust him to stay away. Fools in love were unpredictable. He'd have to see to it that Kennedy wasn't around to mess things up more than he already had.

The odds were that she'd pack up and go home. Unfortunately, he couldn't be sure even then that he would be safe. If she ever started thinking, putting two and two together, remembering...

His lips parted in a wolfish grin, as he remembered how Kennedy had slammed that worthless bodyguard against the side of the car. He'd expected Adams to have someone guarding her, and Kennedy had led him right to the man. He'd thought the guard might be the man in the gray car and Kennedy's assault had convinced him. He'd wait a few minutes and then go over and fix it so he'd never spy on anyone again. Another problem gone.

Placing the earphones on again, he heard the muffled sound of sobs, a chair scraping on a floor, then the sound of a rushing shower. Getting ready for bed— she wouldn't be going anywhere for several hours. It would give him plenty of time to take care of the Kennedy matter. Who knew how much she'd told him? And then, he would take care of her, once and for all....

Chapter Fifteen

Joe Pasco didn't rise when Brian entered his office. Barricaded behind his polished walnut desk, he didn't jump up to grasp Brian's hand as he usually did. Brian wondered if he was still angry because he had slugged him for the comment about Malinche. Their relationship had been strained in the past few days, but Brian still couldn't bring himself to believe the worst about his boss.

Pasco seemed ill at ease, shifting in his seat, fiddling with a pen that Brian knew he rarely used. He used his computer to write; the pen took the place of worry beads.

"Hi, Joe, what's new?"

Pasco finally looked at him, a scowl on his face. When he spoke, his voice dripped sarcasm. "Well, hello, Brian. Glad you could make it in today." He made a show of consulting his watch. "Let's see. I left several messages last night, each one asking you to call me as soon as you got in. It's now 9:00 a.m."

"Isn't that our normal starting time?" Brian crossed the room and flopped down in a chair, his smile as innocent as he could make it. He had considered answering the calls, but he hadn't been in the mood to handle Joe Pasco. Not with Malinche on his mind.

He'd tossed and turned all night, barely able to keep from rushing back and telling her he'd made a horrible mistake. He admitted to himself that he'd been too sensitive about Buck. So the man had hedged his bet, hired others to protect her, too. It made sense. If he, himself, had so easily disarmed one sentry, others could do it, too.

Mostly though, rational thought had nothing to do with it. He ached, he burned, he longed to sink into the velvet of her body, feel her respond like tinder to a match. No matter what happened in the future.

He hadn't gone back, though. He suspected she'd see right through him and realize he still had his doubts about any kind of permanent relationship. She'd know he wasn't expecting forever after. And she'd made it clear she wouldn't accept half measures.

"Besides," he said, jerking his attention back to Joe, "I'm still on vacation, remember?"

Joe didn't smile back. Pouches under his eyes marked his olive skin, and a dark stubble covered his jaw. His white shirt was wrinkled. Had he slept at all?

"I remember that you're on vacation." Pasco rubbed his hand wearily across his chin. "I'm surprised you remember. You don't act much like a man relaxing."

"So, what's so urgent?" Brian crossed his legs at the ankles and tipped the chair back, his thumbs thrust in the pockets of his denims. He knew his mode of dress irritated Joe; Pasco considered them out of place in the office. Brian had chosen them deliberately. He was no happier with his boss than Joe was happy with him. Pasco had some explaining to do. Why had he followed them to Kotzebue, among other things?

Pasco didn't reply directly. "What time did you get back in Anchorage?"

"Oh, late afternoon, I guess. Were you the one who arranged the welcoming committee?"

"So, Buck Adams found you. He was pretty upset when he found out what his daughter was doing."

"But somebody had to tell him, didn't they? He didn't fly up on a whim. Malinche thought it could have been any number of people. I thought it was you."

"Jim Wilson thought Adams should be informed," Joe said stiffly. "Too bad Adams didn't just bundle her up and get her out of here. It would have saved a lot of trouble."

"I don't worry too much about saving people trouble." Brian's lip tightened dangerously. "Any more than someone has been concerned about saving me trouble."

"You're causing it yourself," Joe retorted. "And now you've gone beyond the point where I can help you."

"Help me! Is that what you've been doing, trailing me all through Alaska? Refusing to tell me what's going on? It seems more like spying to me."

"Well, I was trying to help, no matter what you think. If you hadn't been so stubborn, this would have been settled long ago. I warned you to stay out of this Stanislof thing, but you wouldn't listen. Now it's out of my hands."

Brian leaned forward. "About this 'Stanislof thing—'"

"It doesn't matter now. You're out of it," Pasco snapped. "You've been transferred."

"Transferred!" It wasn't the first time a transfer had

been threatened by the higher-ups. Brian was too independent to be a team player, but he was stunned by the timing, and Pasco's agreement. Usually Pasco pulled every string he could to keep Brian where he wanted to be—in Alaska. The suddenness and finality of this order was completely unexpected.

"Isn't this a little sudden? When am I expected to leave?"

Pasco refused to meet his eyes. "As of now you are no longer attached to the Anchorage office. You'll leave here and go directly to the airport." He drew a sheaf of papers from his desk. "Here are the tickets. We've made reservations for you on the flight to Djakarta."

"Indonesia! Right now? It's ridiculous to think I'm going at all, but to expect me to leave on such short notice is insane!"

Pasco spoke as though he were reciting a prepared speech. "Everything will be taken care of. Your belongings will be shipped, or sold if you prefer. But you will leave immediately."

"Like hell I will!" Brian leaped to his feet and planted his hands on the desk. Pasco shrunk back from the fury in his eyes. "What are you trying to pull?"

"Brian, it's the best thing for you," Pasco said, a pleading note in his voice. "You wouldn't drop it—"

"I thought so! I wouldn't voluntarily drop the Stanislof thing, and now you're leaning on me to make sure I do. I wouldn't have expected it of you Joe—we've been friends—"

"And still are. That's why I advise you to be on that plane. This goes way above me—"

"How far?" Brian pounded his fist on the table. "Wilson? The head office?"

"I'm not at liberty to say."

"What about Malinche? How are you going to get rid of her?"

"She's not our concern. Universal Oil doesn't employ Miss Adams," Pasco replied. "She would have been smart to go home with her father. Since she didn't, she'll have to look after herself."

"Do you know how heartless that sounds? You know about the attempts that have been made on her life?"

"Damn it, Brian!" Pasco jumped up from his chair and paced the room. "I did all I could do to protect you! Do you think I like this? You act like this is a game, you poke around, somebody slaps your hands. It's not a game. I know where some of the pressure is coming from, and I can tell you this much, it's nobody I want to mess around with."

"I refuse the transfer."

"You have no choice," Pasco said quietly. "You will leave here immediately, and you will contact no one. It's the best deal I could get for you, Brian. If you don't go, if you decide to go home, I'm not sure you'll even make it that far. Take the transfer."

"No. I don't work for Universal Oil anymore. I quit."

"Brian, think." Pasco leaned toward him, eyes desperate. "Even if they let you live, they'll see that you never work in the oil industry again."

"I can always get a cabin out in the bush and shoot moose. See you around, Joe."

He turned on his heel, glancing back over his shoulder. Pasco was back behind his desk, face gray, looking utterly defeated. Perhaps Pasco really had fought the transfer. It was a sobering thought. If the best Pasco could do was ship him to Indonesia, he had better watch his back.

He took the stairs two at a time. He was still stunned. An hour ago his life was predictable enough. Now, he was unemployed, without a clue as to what to do next.

When Pasco had told him he was to leave without contacting anyone, he had thought first of Malinche. More than thought of her. She had filled his mind, driving out every other concern. To get on a plane, not even say goodbye—it wasn't only ridiculous, it was impossible. Unthinkable.

He rushed out the double doors, looking right and left for anyone who might be lurking in the parking lot. Pasco had hinted he might be attacked before he got home. He felt like a target, darting among the parked cars. He'd never see the assassins if they were here in a vehicle, until they followed him. Or shot him now from the anonymity of a car. Hair prickled on the back of his neck as he hopped in his Jeep. He didn't think in terms of evil auras, as the old shaman did, but he felt something inimical in the air. The killer wouldn't be far away.

He might have a few minutes. Whoever had instigated his transfer expected he would accept it, so there might not have been time to get assassins on his trail yet. He wouldn't have much time, though.

Time for what? To get to Malinche, of course. To head off the danger closing in on her. He wasn't the primary target. Malinche was the instigator, the one who refused to give up. They couldn't persuade her to leave, they couldn't intimidate her. A cold chill settled in his heart. They had only one other option—to kill her.

His hands trembled as he switched on the ignition.

He had to reach her in time. He cursed his pride and stupidity. He had been a complete fool to leave her. He'd been thinking that ever since he left her, but when Pasco told him he was to leave Anchorage without even a chance to say goodbye, he'd known with deep certainty that he couldn't do it. It wasn't even a conscious decision. He had known in the depth of his being that it was simply impossible.

He had fought his love for her, sure it would bring him pain in the future. Pain there might be, but the future without her was worse than pain. It was dark, endless agony. It was living with the knowledge that he'd had a chance for happiness and that cowardice had kept him from seizing it.

Sweat beaded his forehead, and he pressed harder on the accelerator. If it wasn't already too late. He had acted like a jealous child because Buck Adams had left another man to protect her. Now he could only pray that man was competent.

MALINCHE AWOKE that morning with the nagging feeling that something was wrong. Drugged by the sleeping pill, it took a moment for the full remembrance to flood back. She knew what was causing her despair, her feeling that nothing would ever be right again. Brian was gone.

But she wouldn't lie here whining about it; crying never helped. She had some difficult decisions to make. About Brian himself, of course, there was no decision to make. He had made the decision; he was gone. Probably, when she'd had time to think about it, she would realize it was for the best.

Brian had told her to go back to Seattle. He had rejected her. And just as well. His decision was right for her as well as him. Wild passion, even love, wasn't enough to heal the wounds life had dealt them both. She had been diverted, but her real priority was to discover her place in the world.

She would get over Brian. Or maybe she wouldn't, but she could learn to banish his memory to where it wasn't a constant, lacerating pain. As it was now.

What was she going to do about Dimitri? Hadn't she done everything she could, everything any reasonable person would expect? Everyone insisted that she drop it and get on with her life. Possibly they were right.

At a sharp knock on her door, she flung aside the comforter. Tying her robe around her waist, she padded to the door, trying to ignore the sliver of hope that quickened her pulse. Had Brian come back to apologize? She cracked open the door, leaving the chain in place.

Her heart fell. Her landlady, Mrs. Penman, stood outside the door, arms folded across her chest, her scarlet robe contrasting with the improbably blond hair. Malinche had never seen her before without makeup; she had never seen her so outraged before, either.

"Mrs. Penman—"

"I knew I never should have rented to a lone woman." The landlady's tone was as belligerent as her stance. "But you seemed quiet enough. Now, I think I'd better lay down some rules around here."

Malinche repressed her impulse to fire back. "Is something wrong, Mrs. Penman?"

"Is something wrong! It's impossible for anyone to get any sleep around here. Since you've been back from that trip, there's been nothing but one commotion after another. First it was your boyfriend dragging that fellow out of the car and nearly beating him to death. Then there was the argument—''

''Argument?'' Malinche gave the woman a cool look. The only way Mrs. Penman could have known about her and Brian's disagreement was if she'd had her ear up against the wall. ''I'd hardly call a *private* discussion an argument.''

Mrs. Penman blushed at the word *private,* but doggedly held her ground. ''It wasn't so much the argument. I don't appreciate your boyfriend coming around at night, trying to force his way into your apartment.''

''Force his way in!'' Malinche fell back a few steps into her apartment, taking the chain off the hook and opening the door. ''What do you mean?''

Mrs. Penman followed her in. ''Your problems are between yourselves, but I figured if you wanted him in, he'd have a key—not be trying to jimmy the door or tear off the window screen. I didn't get a wink of sleep. I told him anymore of that and I'd call the police.''

All the blood seemed to drain from Malinche's head. She put out a trembling hand to steady herself. Someone had tried to break in. She could have been killed in her drugged sleep.

She rushed to pull back the drapes. What was Buck's sentry doing while this was going on? The gray sedan was parked exactly where it had been the night before. She could make out the outline of the man slumped behind the wheel. He'd probably been asleep all night. Wait until she told Buck about this!

She turned shakily from the window. ''Mrs. Penman, I'm really sorry that your sleep was disturbed. Did you get a look at this man? I don't think it was my—boyfriend.''

"He kept well back in the shadows. I just assumed that was who it was. And I yelled at him through the door—I didn't actually go out in the hall to confront him. I told him I had a gun and that I'm a good shot—which I am. I couldn't identify him."

She shuddered, suddenly looking vulnerable and frail. "I don't mind telling you, even though I didn't get a good look at him, something about him scared me. I heard him cursing and—I wouldn't want a man like that after me. If it *was* you boyfriend, you'd better think twice, dearie."

"He wasn't." But if not Brian, who? The answer was simple. Whoever had been pursuing them for the past week hadn't given up.

There was such a thing as courage. There was also such a thing as stupidity. No one, not even Dimitri, could say she hadn't tried. But she had lost, and now she might lose her life. She'd been lucky so far. How long could blind luck last?

She hadn't been successful at anything, not her relationship with Brian, not with finding her roots, not running down her brother's cold-blooded killer; she was only getting innocent people in trouble. It was time to go home.

There was one last thing she had to do before she went back to Seattle. She spent a few more minutes talking with Mrs. Penman. Then, blinded by tears, she took her suitcase down from the closet shelf.

THE MAN IN the dark van shifted on his seat and scowled, beating his hand rhythmically on the dash. How he would love to get his hands around that busybody landlady's neck. Oh, he'd thought about it, but, as precarious as things were, she wasn't worth the trouble.

Still, the night hadn't been wasted. He had put the pressure on and Kennedy was out of the way. Even if the man knew something, he'd be out of the game in Indonesia. The rest should have been simple; just slide into the woman's room and take care of the loose end.

He hadn't planned to kill her there and have all of Adams's minions after him. A disappearance would do just fine. Lots of suspicions, nothing proven. He knew ways to dispose of a body so it would never be found.

He should have been more careful with disposing of that fool Stanislof. He'd never dreamed anyone would find the body until the elements had done their work. And that other snooping Native, Charlie something. The ice floe should have crushed him beyond recognition and carried him out to sea. And who would have thought Kennedy and the damned girl would be rescued from the ice? He'd been unlucky, and it was past time for a change.

He'd thought it all through carefully before he made his move on Malinche. The man Adams had stationed outside the apartment was so easy to dispose of it was laughable. No one would put up a fuss about a man like him. Then, into the apartment with a needle, drug her unconscious—

But that nosy old woman spoiled everything. Yelling at him, saying she would call the cops. If she had just once stepped out into the hall, he could have silenced her forever.

But it wasn't over yet, not by a long shot. Kennedy was out of the way, and Malinche had to leave the house sometime. When she did, he would dispose of her, and this time he wouldn't miss. And all the land-lady could say was that she left the house on her own.

Suddenly he snapped to attention, a bird dog on point. The door to the apartment opened and Malinche

came swiftly down the walk, carrying a suitcase. A
great stillness came over him, a concentration of pur-
pose, a calm certainty that this was going to be the
time.

He watched her enter her vehicle and back out of
the driveway, then drive down the street. He edged the
van out onto the street and followed about a block
behind her.

BRIAN'S JEEP SCREECHED to a stop in front of
Malinche's apartment. His tension eased as he saw the
gray sedan still parked half a block away. The man,
Jerry Smith, was still here, and he wouldn't be if anything had happened to Malinche. He would be following, calling Adams, something.

Perhaps he should reconnoiter before barging in on
Malinche, and find out if Smith had seen any activity.
As he drew closer, he saw the man was slumped over
the wheel. If the bastard was dozing when he should
be watching, he'd kill him! He strode quickly to the
vehicle and swung open the door.

The man toppled out onto the grass at his feet.

Brian stared down at what had been Jerry Smith. The
man's face was twisted in a horrible grimace, and his
throat was slit nearly ear to ear. Blood—what seemed
like gallons of blood—covered the body, dripped off
onto the green grass where it sparkled like garnets in
the morning sun.

The sight acted like a shot of adrenaline. Brian raced
up the walk, flung open the door, and rushed into the
hallway.

He skidded to a halt in front of her door. It was
closed. He stilled his panting, listening for movement.
Not a sound came from inside the apartment. He tried
the door. Locked.

"Malinche! Malinche! Open up!" Desperate, he pounded on the frame door until it rattled on its hinges.

He'd have to break it down. He had to get to her immediately. If she was hurt or— He tried to keep the possibility out of his mind, but it screamed in defiance. She might be dead.

He didn't hear the door open down the hall, and was hardly aware of the hand pulling sharply on his sleeve, until he heard an angry voice close to his ear.

"Here, now, that's enough of that!"

Dazed, he turned to face a tall blond woman with a formidable expression and a revolver in her hand. He sucked in his breath; it was pointed right at him.

He let his hands fall to his sides. "Where is she? Is she all right?"

The woman took her time scrutinizing him, then slowly lowered the gun. "You must be the boyfriend, not the other one."

"The other one?" Fear fought with frustration, as he waited for her to go on.

"I recognize you. You were the one who dragged that poor fellow out of the car. Miss Adams said you were all right, that it was someone else who tried to break into her place last night."

"Tried to break in?" He clenched his fists, wishing he had someone to hit. "Where is she?"

"Gone."

"Gone?" He'd like to wipe that smug smile off her face, but she was the only one who could give him a clue about what had happened. He took a huge breath, and gave her a charming smile. "Did she happen to say where she was going?"

"Not exactly. But I'm sure she won't be back. She asked me to sell all her stuff."

"Then she must have planned on going back to Seattle.'' He had never known a man could feel so cold, so hopeless. She would be safe there, with Buck to protect her, but it didn't assuage his feeling of utter loneliness, his knowledge that he had missed his chance at happiness. But at least she would be safe.

"I guess so," the landlady said. "She did mention that she had to go someplace else first."

"Where? Did she say where?" He grabbed her arm.

She shook him off. "Not exactly." Her shrewd eyes measured him, as though deciding how much she should tell. Apparently, he passed. "She did ask me what was the best way to get to Ward Cove. I told her probably a flight into Ketchikan, and then a rented car."

Good God, she wasn't safe at all. She might be heading right into the lion's den. He whirled around and headed towards the door.

"There's another thing," the landlady called out, stopping him midstride. "I don't know if it means anything, but a van has been parked in the neighborhood for a couple of days. Didn't belong to the folks who owned the house where it was parked. It pulled out right behind her. It might have been following her."

Brian didn't wait for another word. "There's a body out on the grass," he called over his shoulder. "You'd better call the police."

He was halfway out the door when he heard her sharp intake of breath. He leaped into his Jeep and burned rubber toward his plane.

Chapter Sixteen

Malinche pointed her rented Buick Regal north on the Tongass highway out of Ketchikan on the way to Ward Cove. This bustling development wasn't what she had expected in what had once been a desolate, forsaken stretch of shoreline. She passed the docks where the big cruise ships landed, then a modern shopping center. At Tongass Narrows, she glanced down at a floatplane dock where several small planes rocked restlessly.

The sight reminded her of Brian. Not that he had ever been out of her mind. What would he think when he found her gone? At the time, she'd thought only of fleeing and leaving her problems behind. Perhaps she should have said goodbye, but she didn't think she was capable of it without collapsing in a soggy mess.

Not that it mattered; it might be days before he even knew she was gone. After all, she had asked him to leave. He had taken her at her word, might even be feeling relief. She would forget about him, get on with her life, as soon as she had made this last pilgrimage, this final attempt to reconcile her conflicts. She had to say goodbye to her mother and brother and all they represented.

The area was so built up that she might not even find

the ancient cannery. Perhaps it had long ago been de-
molished. Most of what might have been canneries
were now renovated, modern buildings.

But had they really exorcised the old ghosts, stilled
the long-dead voices? She drove half a mile farther on,
then left her car parked along the road and walked toward the water through a stand of Sitka spruce. Breaking through the undergrowth, she came upon a gap in
the development along the shore: no businesses, no
campgrounds, no monuments. The scene before her
looked just as it might have fifty years ago.

She walked a few feet farther and gazed down on
the sea from the top of a low bluff. The tide was out,
exposing a deserted rocky shoreline that faded into an
expanse of dark gray mud.

But this spot hadn't always been deserted. Her pulse
quickened as she saw the skeleton of an ancient building stretched out toward the sea. Deserted, dilapidated,
it was apparently too far gone to be restored; it remained a solemn monument to the past. Could this be
the site of the original cannery, the forlorn remains of
the building that had housed the displaced Aleuts?

She stood motionless, opening her heart to the feelings that washed over her, willing the past to come
alive. Had her mother, a mere child, scrounged along
that shore for the clams that were all she had to eat?
Had Dimitri, not knowing what the future held, been
there, too? Had the children known each other? The
coincidence wouldn't have been so strange. Most of
the Aleuts had been in the camp. Did she really hear
the muted sound of voices, or was it the wind sobbing
over the water? Such a miasma of sadness rose from
the scene that she raised her hand to brush the tears
from her eyes.

"Yes, it is a place of evil." The voice came from right beside her.

She whirled, clutching her chest. An old man stood there, clothed in the Native dress of the Aleut. Where had he come from? She had been so immersed in thought that she hadn't noticed his approach. Stooped and fragile, his face as wrinkled as a dried apricot, he seemed as ancient and eternal as the tide.

He gazed down at the devastated building. His attention wasn't on her, but on the panorama below.

"You know this place?" She whispered, as though not to disturb the sleeping ghosts.

He nodded. "I know it well. I was among those taken here by the army when the Japanese threatened our homes. The building is mostly gone now—destroyed, like everything else." His voice held no bitterness, only quiet acceptance.

"How horrible that they forced you to leave your home."

"It wasn't done maliciously." He gazed at the remnants of the cannery, seeing something she would never see. "They thought it was for our own good. Then they forgot about us, leaving us here in the cold, with no food. Many died. They had other things on their minds, I guess."

"How can you bear to come back here?"

"My wife died here," he said simply. "I come back often to speak to her. Sometimes she doesn't answer...sometimes I hear her calling in the wind."

His pain was so real, so immediate, that Malinche couldn't find words. Anything she said would sound pretentious, patronizing. For several minutes they stood together staring down at the site of so much past misery.

"Did you know my mother?" she asked finally. "Tara Markof? She would have been just a child. And a young boy, Dimitri Stanislof?"

She waited as the old man thought back through over fifty years of his memory. "Oh, yes," he finally said. "A little girl, Tara. An orphan. We all did what we could but it was hard for everybody. And I remember Dimitri and his mother. Marie, she was called. A beautiful woman. She helped the little girl Tara escape when some Indians wandered close by and agreed to take her. She saved the child's life, I suppose. The odds were that she would starve. And Dimitri, very quiet, very sad. I don't think he spoke a word after his mother was killed."

"Killed?" Her breath seemed to stick in her throat. Was this the evil thing Dimitri had alluded to that had happened at Ward Cove? "What happened?"

"One of the soldiers raped her, then killed her." His even tone lent further horror to his words. "At least, we believed it to be so. The boy was sitting by his mother's ravaged body when we found her. The man was gone."

"But didn't you do something? Report it?"

"Report to who? There was a war going on, many were being killed everywhere. And would they believe us? Or even care?" He shrugged. "Soon after that, the boy slipped away. I don't know where he went. I was just happy he got away. It was hardest on the young."

His cracked old voice ceased, and he stiffened, closing his eyes and lifting his head as though listening to an unknown sound. To Malinche, only the wind howled up from the sea, but he smiled and made his slow way down the side of the bluff without another word. Had he heard his long-lost love in the voice of the wind?

She watched him reach the edge of the sea and get into a seal skin kayak. Stroking the oar strongly, he vanished around a bend.

Malinche stood still, stunned by what she had just learned. Buck had said Tara, her mother, would never speak of the time in the camp. How strangely it had worked out. Tara would have had no way of knowing that the woman who saved her life had been married to the man she would one day marry. Dimitri's mother had saved her own mother. Because of the woman who had been so horribly ravaged and killed, she, Malinche, existed. She owed the woman so much. The horror of what had happened so long ago chilled her to her soul. She could hear the screams, feel the pain....

And her brother had seen it all. Was this rapist and killer the man he had sought for years?

She shivered and crossed her arms tightly across her chest, warding off more than the cold. She had arrived full circle, looking down at the site where her mother's people had been held captive by her father's people, the site of the conflict that beat in her heart still. Only it was so much worse than she'd imagined. Her heart ached for the young child that had been her mother. She had found her, found where it had all started.

And there was nothing she could do, no way she could change the past. But now, seeing where it all began, perhaps she could lay the past to rest and get on with her life.

She couldn't leave them alone without a final farewell. It was the least she could do. Her mother and half brother hadn't died here, but their tragedy had begun here. Some essence of them must linger. She would go down to the beach and say goodbye to her mother, to her brother, two people she had never known, but who each lived on in her.

She scrambled down the rocky trail and walked slowly along the beach. Even in May, the wind off the water was cold. She could imagine that during the winter it must have cut through the flimsy structure like a whip.

A segment of one building was still standing, though it leaned precariously against the force of the wind. There was even a door, although it flopped on one hinge. Gingerly, she opened the door, and peered inside.

She stared into the barrel of a blue-steel Walther pistol.

She froze, unable to tear her eyes from the weapon. She couldn't scream, couldn't move. Finally, with tremendous effort, she lifted her gaze to the man who held the pistol pointed so steadily at her heart.

She looked into the deadliest, most reptilian eyes she had ever seen, eyes of a cold, lifeless blue.

She recognized him at once; Brian had described him perfectly. Carl Bettnor. The man who had identified himself to Brian as a CIA agent. As blood flowed back into her veins, she opened her mouth to scream, but the steady way he held the pistol made her think twice.

He jerked the pistol a fraction of an inch, indicating she should step inside. "Well, Miss Adams, at last we meet face-to-face. Although that's not quite correct. I've met you—you just weren't conscious at the time." His chuckle was like his eyes, void of human feeling.

She wouldn't give him the pleasure of seeing how

frightened she was. "You're Carl Bettnor. You killed Dimitri."

"Of course."

"But why? Why was the CIA interested? He wasn't a spy."

The comment seemed to amuse him. "Of course he wasn't. But he couldn't be allowed to live. Any more than you can. I'm sorry it took so long. You should have died weeks ago when I tried to run you over. Certainly you should have perished on the ice. You lead a charmed life—but your luck just ran out."

He was deadly serious. She was about to be killed and she didn't even know why. Her words came in a rush.

"But I don't understand! Why? I've done nothing—"

"Except to dig around in what was none of your business."

Anger stiffened her spine. He had no right. He had already taken too much from her. Never to see Brian or Buck again, all because of this murderer. How dare he? "You can't get away with it. When they find my body, nothing in the world will keep them from tracking you down."

"You disappoint me, Miss Adams. You've shown a lot of nerve and intelligence up to now, but that comment—it's so cliché—'you can't get away with it.' Of course I can. When—if—they find you, they'll think it was another accident."

She glanced at the gun. "But an accident? With a bullet hole in me?"

"You underestimate me. I would have thought of something to do with your body, but you made it so easy, coming here. Are you familiar with this coast?

When the tide is out, stretches of the mud flats are like a huge suction cup. Anything that stumbles in there stays. It's impossible to get out. Nearly every summer, some stupid person gets caught in the mud.''

She cast a panic-stricken glance at the tide flat, narrower now than it had been a few minutes ago.

''They don't sink all the way. Not completely, not right away, that is. But there's no way to get them out. Struggling just sinks them deeper. A force strong enough to get them out would pull them apart. Not much use pulling half out if the other half is still stuck.'' He chuckled, that mirthless chuckle, that frightened her more than the gun. ''You'll just be stuck there until the tide comes in and then you'll drown.''

He glanced over his shoulder. ''The tide turned a while ago. A few minutes, and it should be just right. If they ever recover your body, there won't be a bullet hole in it. You'll be just another tourist who stumbled out too far and couldn't get back.''

The full horror of her situation only now began to penetrate her shock. He meant it. Without compunction, he would arrange this terrible death. She had to fight, stall for time. She said the first thing that came to her mind.

''How did you know you'd find me here?''

''I've been following you since you left Anchorage. When you and the old Eskimo were talking, I figured you'd come on down for a look-see. I just beat you to it.''

''Who are you really? You aren't CIA.''

''Oh, yes I am. Why else do you think that fool Joe Pasco was so accommodating? He was convinced national security was at stake.'' His laugh sent shivers down her spine.

"Tell me why. If Dimitri wasn't a spy, why did you kill him? If you're going to kill me, I deserve to know the reason."

He glanced over his shoulder again. "It will be a few more minutes before the tide is right. Why not?"

He shifted his bulk to rest one hip on an exposed timber. Could she make a run for it? No way. He would kill her before she'd gone two steps. Might not that be better than the death he had planned for her? But she wouldn't give up yet. There had to be a chance...

"I was a soldier here at Ward Cove," he said. "I was just a kid. Seventeen. My whole unit was out fighting Japs, and I'm stuck here guarding a bunch of gooks. Not too bad-looking, some of them, though. The one woman put up a fight, and I had to kill her. Bad luck. The kid was watching, he screamed—well, I couldn't just hang around."

"Dimitri?"

"Yeah. I left and rejoined my unit. They didn't ask questions. It was the biggest battle of the war for them, so they were glad to have me back. After the war I knocked around awhile, then joined the CIA. I climbed up through the ranks. No problem. I'm in line for a political appointment, the top of the heap. I can't afford even a hint of scandal."

"But what harm could Dimitri do after so long?"

"Yeah, that's what I thought. I never gave him another thought. He was just a kid. No way he could finger me. Then a letter from some guy named Stanislof came in to the Department of the Army. He wanted to know the name of a soldier who had been at Ward Cove. Good thing I had a contact. He told me right away. I never knew the kid's name, but I didn't like it that somebody in Alaska was asking about a soldier at Ward Cove. I had my contact write back, giving a phony name. I decided I'd better come up and see what was going on.''

"The letter was from Dimitri. You wondered if he was remembering things?"

"Yeah. And I no sooner stepped off the plane than I knew I was right. Right there in the airport for tourists to pick up was a damned dragon."

"But what had his carved dragons to do with anything? He'd always carved them, ever since he was a child."

Shifting the gun to his other hand, but still pointing it at her, he unbuttoned his shirt and pulled it aside.

She gasped. Emblazoned across Bettnor's chest was a huge tattoo of a dragon.

"He remembered," she whispered. "He saw it when you raped his mother, and subconsciously, he remembered."

"I had to find out how much he remembered," Bettnor said. "I followed him to the Eskimo Gathering, and got acquainted. He still didn't know too much—he was following up on a phony name—but I saw from the last dragon he carved that things were coming back. Then he came to the sauna one night, and I was there—"

"And he saw the tattoo—and he knew."

Bettnor glanced at the tide creeping relentlessly to shore. "Come on. Time to go."

"Wait! One more question. With Dimitri dead, what was so dangerous about the dragon? Why did you have to get it away from me? What danger was I when you had it?"

"You would have known if you looked closely at the dragon."

"I did look closely. It was just a dragon."

He took the tiny carving from his pocket and handed it to her. It took a few seconds, and then her eyes opened wide. She had sensed the dragon was somehow different, although she couldn't put her finger on it. Now, staring at the dragon and back at Bettnor's square face with the dead eyes, she saw it. The miniature face, in spite of the forked tongue, the scales on the head, bore a striking resemblance to Carl Bettnor.

"You see?" he said, watching her expression register understanding. "My face was in Dimitri's subconscious, drifting ever closer to the surface. You would have noticed it sooner or later. Probably sooner, since with the political appointment my picture would have been in all the papers. Even when you didn't have it, it might have been in your subconscious, and you would have remembered, like Dimitri did."

"I'm not the only one who saw it. Brian did. He'll remember and come after you."

"Your boyfriend is halfway to Indonesia by now. Don't count on him to rescue you."

She hadn't thought she could feel any worse, but she did. She felt numb, unable to move. Brian in Indonesia. He had actually left her? She had counted on him, hoped he would find her in time. But Brian had left her without a word.

"Move!" He grasped her roughly by the arm, twisting it behind her back, and forcing her along the beach. Pain ran like hot fire through her arm, but still she struggled. She would not die like this, die on a cold, isolated shore. What right had this monster to cut off her life as though he were snapping off a flower? As he had done to Marie so long ago.

The thought gave her strength. Pure fury raged

through her blood. She might die, but she wouldn't go down without a fight.

But with the gun against her head, what could she do?

She struck out with her foot, hoping to make him stumble. He merely twisted her arm harder, increasing the pressure until she nearly blacked out, as he angled her toward the strip of mud.

BRIAN SLAMMED on the brakes. His heart pounded. Two vehicles were parked along the shoulder of the road. One was hers. It matched the description given at the rental agency. Whose was the other?

There was no one near the cars. She must have walked through the tangle of trees toward the shoreline, toward the remnants of Ward Cove.

Absolute terror pumped adrenaline through his every artery. Brian vaulted from the vehicle, fought his way through the thin line of trees, and dashed to the low bluff that loomed above Ward Cove. If the killer had tracked her down, he would squash her like a fly. Brian had to be in time, he had to be!

How could a man be so stupid? To have love in his hand, and let it go because he was afraid he would not have it forever.

When he broke through the trees, what he saw froze his heart in his chest. Two figures struggled at the edge of the ocean. He didn't need his eyes to see who it was; his heart recognized Malinche.

Pure fury blazed through him, along with desperate fear. Catapulting from the bank, he hit the beach running. Gravel crunched beneath his feet, seaweed tore at his legs. He took the cold wind into his lungs in deep, rasping gulps. If the man forced her deeply into the mud, it would be impossible to free her. He had to get there in time!

The man's back was turned to Brian, all his attention on the woman as they struggled at the edge of the mud.

Hold on, sweetheart, hold on! I'm coming!

He didn't say the words aloud, but over her attacker's shoulder, Malinche glanced up. Her eyes met his. A look of wild joy lit her face. A current arced across the space, touched both of them. The contact burned into his soul, fusing them together. It was primitive, elemental, on a level below mind or will. She was his woman and she was in deadly danger.

He hadn't known he could run any faster, but he did. Thank God the sound of the incoming tide covered his footsteps crunching the rocks and his harsh, gasping breath. One more minute...

Malinche twisted in Bettnor's grasp, and aimed a kick at his crotch. Bettnor swore, taking the gun from her head, as he shoved her toward the tideline. He still held her arm as she stumbled backward.

Still several feet away, Brian gathered all his strength and launched himself at the man. He managed to grab him around the knees. The force of his attack knocked Bettnor off balance.

Startled, Bettnor stumbled, releasing his hold on Malinche. In an instant, he regained his feet. Snarling, he whirled, gun in hand. Brian leaped up from a crouch, swinging as he came.

Perhaps it was the surprise, perhaps it was some reserve Brian didn't know he had. He knocked the gun from Bettnor's hand.

Malinche gazed wildly around, searching for a way to help Brian. The gun lay on the beach; she scooped it up, then realized it was useless. She couldn't shoot without the possibility of hitting Brian. As she circled, looking for a clear shot, Brian delivered a stunning blow to Bettnor's jaw. Off balance, Bettnor stumbled backward—into the black muck that grabbed at his feet like a hungry monster.

Bettnor froze, as the enormity of what had happened penetrated his mind. Eyes rimmed with terror, he stared down at his feet. Already the black ooze was up to his ankles. As panic took hold, he struggled. He took a step, only to sink deeper into the remorseless quick-sand.

Horrified, Malinche and Brian stared wordlessly as each attempted step forced him deeper into the ooze. Impulsively, Brian leaned toward him and held out his hand. Bettnor stretched toward it, but several feet separated the two. Brian dared not get closer, or he would be imprisoned by the mud himself.

"We've got to get help." Malinche couldn't take her eyes from the muck into which Bettnor was inexorable sinking.

Brian swallowed. He hated this man, he would gladly have killed him, but the death that awaited Bettnor was more than he would have wished anyone. "I think it's too late."

Already the black mud was above Bettnor's knees. The trapped man looked down at his vanishing legs and gave a high-pitched scream—a scream that would linger in Brian's mind forever.

"We've got to try!" Malinche tugged at his shirt.

"I think your boyfriend is right. I'll send for help, but they'll never get here in time." A quiet voice spoke from directly behind them.

Brian whirled. "Jim Wilson! Where did you come from?"

Wilson ignored him as he spoke briefly into a cellular phone. Then he moved to stand beside them, his eyes on Bettnor. The blood seemed to drain from his face, as he watched the man who had now ceased to struggle.

He shook his head as if throwing off a nightmare. When he spoke, his voice was calm and controlled. "I've been after Bettnor for a long time, but I hate to see anyone die like that."

"How did you know he was here?" Malinche averted her eyes from the doomed man.

"And who are you?" Brian asked.

"I figured that all I had to do was stick close to you two and I'd find him. As to who I am—" He flipped credentials from his pocket. "CIA."

"Then you knew about what he did in camp?" Malinche asked.

"No, but there have been other suspicious things. Leaks where there shouldn't have been any, agents betrayed. We began to suspect him a while ago, but never anything specific."

"But he was in line for a political appointment!"

Wilson smiled grimly. "Not until our investigation was complete, but of course he didn't know that."

Bettnor had stopped screaming. He gazed at them now with the resigned eyes of an animal. It was a horrible fate, even if he had planned the same for Malinche. Brian tried to turn her away, but she stood squeezing his hand as though it were a lifeline. Touching her, knowing she was safe, made it somewhat easier to watch the horror in front of them.

Sirens wailed in the distance, a fire truck screamed to a stop at the top of the cliff, but by that time water lapped serenely over Bettnor's head.

Epilogue

Brian and Malinche lay on Brian's bed, moist and languid from lovemaking that was sweeter each time. His bed was narrow but more than adequate; they didn't need much room.

"Are you sure you don't mind all the fuss of a formal wedding?" Malinche adjusted her head into the curve of his arm.

"As long as you're there, we can be married in an igloo."

"Not scared?" Malinche teased. "It's a big commitment."

Brian kissed the hollow at the base of her throat. "It was never *my* commitment that worried me, sweetheart."

"I know. You didn't trust *me*."

"Forgive me. I know better now."

"You'd better." Her face became serious. "Dad's adamant that the wedding be in Seattle, and a rather formal affair, I'm afraid."

"Don't worry, I'm not about to cross Buck in this. There will be plenty of other things to fight about. And I look great in a tux."

"You look great in nothing, too." Malinche nuzzled

Brian's ear. She couldn't have been happier. They had returned to Anchorage a week ago, leaving Wilson to sort things out in Ketchikan, and had gone straight to Brian's apartment. She was still recovering from the shock of the past few weeks, but telephone calls to her father, and making plans with Brian were having their effect. Now she felt the sublime serenity of a woman who has been well and truly loved.

"As to the wedding, I want whatever you want." His husky voice sent ripples of desire along her veins. "Always."

"I'd like the show and the drama of a big wedding. It's like icing on a cake," she admitted. "Dad won't be happy without it. And I don't feel the need to rebel just to rebel anymore. Besides, he's been so reasonable."

"Considering his only daughter has consented to live in Alaska as the wife of a mere geologist, I'd say he has. Not that he liked it." Brian grinned, remembering the fireworks that had followed that announcement. "I really had to talk fast to escape being head honcho of one of his companies." A shadow crossed his face. "What about you, love? Are you sure? When we first met you had so many conflicts about where you belonged."

"I learned something from Ward Cove." She moved to lay her head on his chest, listening to the strong steady thud of his heart. "The past is just that—past. I don't have to identify with any one culture. I am who I am, and I finally know who that is—the woman who loves you. I know where my home is—it's with you, wherever you are." She gave him a playful punch in the shoulder. "But it certainly took you long enough to learn that."

He caught her hand and raised it to his lips. He'd finally realized that love came with no guarantees; when love came, you grasped it and trusted in the future. "I never realized I was such a slow learner. I loved you from the first moment I saw you, but I was so obsessed with the fact that we were from two different worlds, that you couldn't face up to my life, that I tried to drive you away."

"You'll never get away from me."

"I believe you, with all my heart. And I will never shut you out again. It would be like shutting out my soul."

Brian placed his finger under chin, and tilted her head so he could look into her eyes. "Darling, is it really all right if Joe Pasco is best man? He's trying so hard to make amends." Brian wouldn't mention his own soul-searching; his decision to forget Joe's comments about Malinche. Joe had been under extreme pressure and said things he hadn't meant.

"Of course. And it wasn't really his fault. Carl Bettnor was very persuasive, and he *was* CIA. He just had his own agenda. Joe was in a quandary between his friendship for you and his love for his country."

"He did try his best for me. Even that threatened transfer was to save my life."

"I still don't understand about Jim Wilson," she said.

"Apparently the CIA have been suspicious of Bettnor for some time—too many plans backfiring, too many agents dying. When Bettnor came to Alaska, Wilson was sent by the CIA to watch him without Bettnor's knowledge. Pasco thought Wilson really was a Universal Oil man."

He saw the shadow of pain in her eyes. "What is it, love?"

"Bettnor—the terrible way he died. I know it might

be called poetic justice, but it was so horrible. I wouldn't have wished it on anyone, even him.''

He put his finger gently on her lips. "Try not to think of it. That part's over. Just remember that thanks to you, Dimitri is vindicated, and the perpetrator of an old crime finally received justice.''

She snuggled closer. "And the new part—the best part—the rest of our lives is just beginning.''

Take 2 bestselling love stories FREE

Plus get a FREE surprise gift!

Special Limited-Time Offer

Mail to Harlequin Reader Service®

3010 Walden Avenue
P.O. Box 1867
Buffalo, N.Y. 14240-1867

YES! Please send me 2 free Harlequin Intrigue® novels and my free surprise gift. Then send me 4 brand-new novels every month. Bill me at the low price of $3.34 each plus 25¢ delivery and applicable sales tax, if any.* That's the complete price, and a saving of over 10% off the cover prices—quite a bargain! I understand that accepting the books and gift places me under no obligation ever to buy any books. I can always return a shipment and cancel at any time. Even if I never buy another book from Harlequin, the 2 free books and the surprise gift are mine to keep forever.

181 HEN CH7J

Name _____ (PLEASE PRINT)

Address _____ Apt. No. _____

City _____ State _____ Zip _____

This offer is limited to one order per household and not valid to present Harlequin Intrigue® subscribers. *Terms and prices are subject to change without notice.
Sales tax applicable in N.Y.

UINT-98 ©1990 Harlequin Enterprises Limited

What do you want for Christmas?

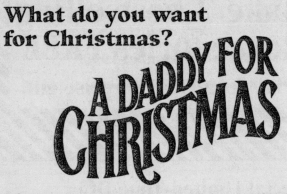

A DADDY FOR CHRISTMAS

'Tis the season for wishes and dreams that come true. This November, follow three handsome but lonely Scrooges as they learn to believe in the magic of the season when they meet the *right* family, in *A Daddy for Christmas*.

MERRY CHRISTMAS, BABY
by Pamela Browning

THE NUTCRACKER PRINCE
by Rebecca Winters

THE BABY AND THE BODYGUARD
by Jule McBride

Available November 1998
wherever Harlequin and Silhouette books are sold.

HARLEQUIN®
Makes any time special ™

Silhouette®

Look us up on-line at: http://www.romance.net

PHBR1198

For a limited time, Harlequin and Silhouette have an offer you just can't refuse.

In November and December 1998:

BUY **ANY** TWO HARLEQUIN
OR SILHOUETTE BOOKS and
SAVE $10.00
off future purchases

OR BUY ANY THREE HARLEQUIN OR SILHOUETTE BOOKS
AND **SAVE $20.00** OFF FUTURE PURCHASES!

(each coupon is good for $1.00 off the purchase of two
Harlequin or Silhouette books)

··

JUST BUY 2 HARLEQUIN OR SILHOUETTE BOOKS, SEND US YOUR
NAME, ADDRESS AND 2 PROOFS OF PURCHASE (CASH REGISTER
RECEIPTS) AND HARLEQUIN WILL SEND YOU A COUPON BOOKLET
WORTH **$10.00 OFF** FUTURE PURCHASES OF HARLEQUIN OR
SILHOUETTE BOOKS IN 1999. SEND US 3 PROOFS OF PURCHASE AND
WE WILL SEND YOU 2 COUPON BOOKLETS WITH A TOTAL **SAVING OF**
$20.00. (ALLOW 4-6 WEEKS DELIVERY) OFFER EXPIRES
DECEMBER 31, 1998.

··

I accept your offer! Please send me a coupon booklet(s), to:

NAME: _____

ADDRESS: _____

CITY: _____ STATE/PROV.: _____ POSTAL/ZIP CODE: _____

Send your name and address, along with your cash register
receipts for proofs of purchase, to:

In the U.S.	In Canada
Harlequin Books	Harlequin Books
P.O. Box 9057	P.O. Box 622
Buffalo, NY	Fort Erie, Ontario
14269	L2A 5X3

PHQ4982

Lost & Found

All new...and filled with the mystery and romance you love!

SOMEBODY'S BABY
by Amanda Stevens in November 1998

A FATHER FOR HER BABY
by B. J. Daniels in December 1998

A FATHER'S LOVE
by Carla Cassidy in January 1999

It all begins one night when three women go into labor in the same Galveston, Texas, hospital. Shortly after the babies are born, fire erupts, and though each child and mother make it to safety, there's more than just the mystery of birth to solve now....

Don't miss this *all new* LOST & FOUND trilogy!

Available at your favorite retail outlet.

HARLEQUIN®
Makes any time special ™